Everyone had their secrets but this one changed everything.

He shook his head as he studied the photo. Numbness took over and his heart constricted.

"What are you doing in here?" Avery's voice from the door shook him loose and he looked up, meeting her gaze, seeing her fear.

He didn't know what to say to her. Even if he had the words, he didn't know if he could speak.

"Give me the picture." She reached to take it from him.

He pulled back, keeping the frame from her grasp. Her eyes widened as she realized he knew the truth.

"Please, Grayson," she said with a trembling voice. "Please give me the picture."

"Give me my daughter," he countered.

"She isn't…"

He cut her off with a shake of his head and he held on to the photo. A photo of Avery and a little girl. A little girl with dark eyes and dark hair, the light catching flecks of auburn. A little girl with his dimples.

Brenda Minton lives in the Ozarks with her husband, children, cats, dogs and strays. She is a pastor's wife, Sunday-school teacher, coffee addict and is sleep deprived. Not in that order. Her dream to be an author for Harlequin started somewhere in the pages of a romance novel about a young American woman stranded in a Spanish castle. Her dreams came true, and twenty-plus books later, she is an author hoping to inspire young girls to dream.

Books by Brenda Minton

Love Inspired

Her Small Town Secret

Mercy Ranch

Reunited with the Rancher
The Rancher's Christmas Match
Her Oklahoma Rancher
The Rancher's Holiday Hope
The Prodigal Cowboy
The Rancher's Holiday Arrangement

Bluebonnet Springs

Second Chance Rancher
The Rancher's Christmas Bride
The Rancher's Secret Child

Visit the Author Profile page at Harlequin.com for more titles.

Her Small Town Secret

Brenda Minton

LOVE INSPIRED

INSPIRATIONAL ROMANCE

LOVE INSPIRED®
INSPIRATIONAL ROMANCE

Recycling programs
for this product may
not exist in your area.

ISBN-13: 978-1-335-48891-6

Her Small Town Secret

Copyright © 2021 by Brenda Minton

This edition published by arrangement with Harlequin Books S.A.

For questions and comments about the quality of this book, please contact us
at CustomerService@Harlequin.com.

Love Inspired
22 Adelaide St. West, 40th Floor
Toronto, Ontario M5H 4E3, Canada
www.Harlequin.com

Printed in U.S.A.

It is of the Lord's mercies that we are
not consumed, because his compassions fail not.
They are new every morning:
great is thy faithfulness.
—*Lamentations* 3:22–23

This book is dedicated to the friends and family who have kept me going through the writing process. Thank you for the prayers, the support and the time.

Chapter One

The door to room 204 in the Pleasant Residential Care center squeaked open. Avery Hammons glanced that way but didn't greet the visitor. She finished taking the vitals of her patient, then gave the redhead at the door a questioning look.

"There's an incredibly gorgeous cowboy waiting for you at the front lobby. He might be all hat and no cattle, but I'd take him if I wasn't happily engaged." Assistant to the administrator of Pleasant Residential Care, Laura Anderson, winked.

"Gorgeous cowboy type?" Avery asked after settling her patient's arm back on her bed. She smiled down at the woman, hoping to reassure her. "Margie, your pulse is strong and your blood pressure is better than that of most twenty-year-olds. In another month you'll be back to walking Dudley in the park."

Margie Duncan drooped a little, her mouth pulling down in a slight frown. That look had become one of her few signs of discontentment. She'd been a model patient in the four weeks she'd been at the facility, recovering from a fractured hip. "I'm so sorry for making a fuss. I just felt a little funny when I got up a bit ago. You're probably right about being anxious. And I can't wait to get home to that silly dog."

The same silly dog who had wrapped a leash around Margie and tripped her as she went down the front steps of her house a month ago. Avery smiled past the worry she felt for her patient. As a supervising RN, worry was a big part of her job.

"You don't have to apologize, Margie. That's what I'm here for. Also, you could have your daughter bring Dudley in for a visit. I won't tell."

"Could I really?" Margie's face lit up at the mention of her poodle.

"I don't see why not."

From the door, Laura cleared her throat. "About the visitor…"

The last thing Avery wanted was a visitor. Especially a male visitor. The only man she could think of was Tucker Church. They'd been on a few dates, nothing serious. She doubted he would visit her at work, especially since she'd made it clear they were just friends and would remain friends. Avery doubted she would ever be at a place in her life where she let someone be more than a friend. It seemed trite to say but she was content with her life as it was. She had a job she loved, people in her life whom she loved and she was building the home she'd always dreamed of. Why complicate things?

Fortunately, Tucker, as a friend, knew her and her past. He knew her heartaches and her secrets. That made it easy to explain to him why she wasn't keen on new relationships.

"You'd best get out there to your visitor," Margie encouraged.

Avery winked at the older woman. "Guess I have to go see who this amazing visitor is and what they need with me. What does it mean, all hat and no cattle?"

Margie laughed at that. "That means he looks like he might be a cowboy but he's probably never seen a cow in his life. I bet he has a pair of shiny boots that ain't ever kicked up the dirt, and a hat that sits on top of his head like a city feller."

"Gotcha." She turned to Laura. "Do we know why our cattle-less visitor is here?"

Laura smirked a bit. "Community service. He said the law grabbed him on his way into town and gave him an ultimatum. Jail or community service that he failed to serve eleven years ago."

"Eleven years ago?"

"Yeah, I guess they aren't aware of the statute of limitations. Nevertheless, he said he's here to work off his service and Mr. Davis told him to see you, that you would oversee his time. Forty hours, just ten hours a week."

"Wonderful, just what I need. I don't have time to babysit a *city feller* who broke the law nearly a dozen years ago."

"Avery Hammons, please come to the front desk. Avery, please come to the front desk." A male voice, not one of their staff, called over the intercom.

"Who was that?" Avery asked, leaving Margie's room, Laura hot on her heels.

"My guess is that would be our man, Mr. All Hat. Can we keep him? Please tell me we can keep him."

Laura practically gushed and she wasn't typically the gushing type.

Avery hurried down the hall of the west wing of the facility, turning a corner and then stopping so quickly, Laura nearly ran into her. "Oh no!"

The cowboy leaned against the counter, the intercom phone in his hand. One corner of his mouth hitched up as he nudged his hat back a smidge. "Honey, I'm home."

No, no, no. Avery stood there in the center of the hall, caught in a nightmare in which Grayson Stone was the star. He was the one person who could—and would—shake up her life and ruin everything. It was what he'd always done. What he did best. He knew how to make her feel beautiful and worthless, all at the same time.

She shook her head, wanting, needing to wake up and have him gone. She closed her eyes, said a quick prayer and opened her eyes slowly.

"I'm still here," he drawled with a slight chuckle as he set the phone on the desk and straightened.

Yes, he was still there. All six feet, lean athletic build of him. He grinned, as if this was all a big joke and he wasn't pushing her life off its foundation. Life had always been a joke to Grayson. The spoiled son of a judge and a pediatrician, he'd always been given everything he ever wanted or needed. He was her exact opposite. She'd been serious, studious, determined to change her future. She had wanted to prove that a kid from Dillon's Trailer Park could become something, someone.

Grayson was her kryptonite.

Eleven years. Had he thought of her even once in all that time? Going by the lack of phone calls, return visits to Pleasant, or even a card, she guessed he hadn't given her a single, solitary thought. He hadn't thought about Pleasant, about her, about that summer.

She had thought about him. Every. Single. Day. And not always pleasant thoughts.

Since her return to town six months ago, she had been working on her relationship with God, seeking a closer walk. But this made her question everything. Why now? Why did Grayson have to show up here just when she finally had her life on track? She had a plan. She had a path forward.

"Ah, now, come on, Avery, that isn't the greeting I expected from you."

She stared at him, unable to speak. Grayson Stone always managed to jerk the rug out from under her. He had a way of turning her inside out. He'd been doing it for as long as she could remember. Probably since kindergarten, when he'd given her a daisy and then tossed a spider on her as she bent her head to smell the flower.

"You're still mad at me, aren't you?" he asked. He wore his customary grin, one he probably practiced in the mirror.

Mad was an understatement. He'd left town without warning, without a goodbye. He'd made promises, then left her sitting at Tilly's Diner, waiting for him to show up.

She studied him, looking for a hint of insecurity. Anything to tell her he might be a little unsure, a little bit sorry. Was there a hint of regret in his brown eyes? Had she seen a flash of something, maybe remorse, on his face just before he pasted on that too-flashy smile?

If he could pretend the past didn't matter, so could she. It might not be easy, but she could do it.

"Why would I be mad at you, Grayson?" she said, like it was all water under the bridge.

"Oh, no reason I can think of, darlin'." He grinned and winked, not at her but at Laura, who stood nearby.

"Why are you here?" Avery asked. Her heart faltered at the one answer that made sense.

But he couldn't know. She told herself to breathe deep and stay calm.

He pushed away from the desk and she was reminded why he'd always been able to take her breath away. Because he was tall and powerful but he didn't steal the room. He moved with an athletic grace. His dark brown auburn hair, combined with suntanned skin and coffee-brown eyes that took on a hint of the forest with flecks of green and gold, were a lethal combination.

Her gaze dropped to his fancy polished leather boots. A giggle worked its way up. Mr. All Hat and No Cattle.

"Do you have an office?" he asked in a voice that no longer teased.

"Yes." She pointed down the hall. "Second door on the right."

He led the way. She drew in a breath and followed, ignoring the questioning looks of her coworkers.

Grayson Stone was home. Avery should have known this day would come like a thief in the night, taking her by surprise, upending everything she'd been trying to do right with her life.

She just didn't think it would come so soon.

Grayson followed Avery into her office. The sign on the door read Supervising RN. The room was barely big enough for the desk, bookcase and utilitarian gray filing cabinet. His attention shifted back to the woman he sure hadn't thought to see again. Ever. He especially hadn't expected to see her here, today. Her green eyes had shot daggers at him when she'd come around the corner of the hallway and spotted him.

He smiled, thinking about that look she'd given him. With her long blond hair pulled back in a ponytail and wearing teddy bear scrubs, she had certainly looked all sweet and nurse-like. But the look she'd given him had carried a pretty specific message, and it had been anything but sweet.

He shouldn't have expected anything more from her. They'd been frenemies for a long time.

Since kindergarten. He cringed at the memory of tossing a spider in her pale blond hair. Yeah, that hadn't been his best move.

Maybe if he apologized and told her he'd changed, she might forgive him. For the spider, for high school, for the way he'd left town years ago. He'd done a lot of people wrong, including Avery. But the decision to leave Pleasant had been made for him.

In the tiny office she slid past him, a soft shoulder nudging his, the scent of clean soap and lavender shampoo wafting in the air between them. She didn't appear to be in a forgiving mood. Sliding out her chair, she pushed a framed photo out of his line of sight and switched into professional mode, suddenly acting as if they didn't share a past.

He took the chair shoved in the corner of her office. His attention strayed to a plant on her desk. Its leaves were wilted and begging for water.

She sat across from him. "Why?"

He shifted his attention back to Avery. He somehow summoned up a smile even though he felt like a fifteen-year-old version of himself, sitting in the principal's office waiting for his dad to come pick him up.

"There are a lot of answers to that question. Where do you want me to start?" he asked without smiling, since she didn't appear to be in the mood for humor.

"Why are you at my place of employment? We can start with that."

"I might have run my car over the flower beds and brick sign before I left town."

"Who does that?"

He raised his hand. "That would be me. My last night in Pleasant might not have been my best. I left a trail of destruction all the way to Springfield where they finally caught me and threw me in jail. I went before a judge who decided I needed to pay for my crimes and to have a change of scenery."

Change of scenery. That left out a lot of details, but what was he supposed to say to her? Should he start with an introduction, the way he had in countless meetings over the past eleven years? Perhaps show her the coin he carried in his pocket, the one he sometimes had to reach for, to remind himself that it felt good to be clean.

"I didn't know," she said, the words not meaning all that much. Of course she hadn't known.

"My dad was pretty good at keeping family secrets." Grayson shrugged, as if it didn't matter.

"What was the change of scenery?" she asked.

"They sent me to California where I eventually went to work for my uncle's contracting business."

"I hope he made you work until you had blisters on your hands."

He held up calloused hands. "See for yourself. I've

spent the past eleven years working hard and learning a lot of life lessons, compliments of my uncle Edward."

"And now you're home?"

"For a couple of months. I'm here to help get my dad resettled on the farm. He's been in rehab in Springfield since his stroke in January. They sent him home at the beginning of May and I got here as quickly as I could."

"I wondered where he'd gone after selling the house in town."

"Springfield. He and my mother moved to Springfield. After she passed away, he moved into a retirement community. But now, because he's sixty-five and had a pretty serious stroke, he wants to be here, in the town he considered his home for most of his life. Since they sold our house in town, he's moving to his old family farm."

She shuffled papers on her desk, ignoring him. That gave him a moment to study her, to study the cubbyhole she called her office, and to wonder about the photograph she clearly didn't want him to see.

"What am I supposed to do with you?" she finally asked.

"I don't know. I'll be here five hours a day, two days a week for the next month."

"I'd rather you not be here at all. Why don't we call it good and you leave?"

"You want me gone?" He winked as he said it.

"California, you said? I'm sure it's nice there in the spring."

"Yes, central coast. Perfect weather every day. Unfortunately, I'm not going anywhere. I'll leave in July at the earliest. And thanks to you, I'm more determined than ever to repay my debt to society," he said with a grin, then winked at her, enjoying the way a flush of pink crept into her cheeks.

He couldn't remember a time that he hadn't loved that blush of hers. Even as a kid he'd been smitten by the flush of pink that had swept through her cheeks at the slightest hint of bashfulness.

This new adult version of Avery was a bit more confident than when Grayson knew her, and seemed to compose herself in a matter of seconds. "Fine, I'm sure we can find something for you to do around here. You can report in the morning…"

"Mornings won't work. I'm at the old homestead and there are livestock to feed." He used the term *livestock* loosely. She didn't need the whole truth. "I also have to make sure my dad eats breakfast before I head out."

"Could you at least be here by ten?" she asked.

"I can be here at ten."

She nodded and walked out of the office, leaving him to follow behind. He stood, giving the room one last look, trying to learn something about the woman she'd become. The wilted plant, a bookcase of medical books, a metal filing cabinet circa 1980, didn't tell him much. He wondered if she'd ever married. He hadn't looked at her ring finger.

He reached for the photo she'd pushed aside when she'd sat down at her desk.

"Put that down. You have no business going through my personal belongings." She stood in the doorway, her face pale, her brilliant green eyes a stark contrast.

Moving quickly, she grabbed the framed picture before he could even touch it.

"What are you hiding, Avery?"

"I'm not hiding anything," she said with a tremor.

His gaze dropped to her hands, still clutching the photograph. No rings. Maybe she'd been widowed? Divorced? If he'd kept in contact with old friends, maybe he'd know more about her life.

The frozen expression on her face told him she wouldn't give him any answers, not today. And he didn't deserve any. He didn't deserve secrets or confidences, either.

As a kid he'd been entitled and spoiled, never understanding the differences in their lives. She'd been a pretty loner in hand-me-down clothes who had spent her time studying. That last summer in Pleasant, he'd come home from his first year of college and he'd taken a good look at his childhood nemesis and he'd seen her, really seen her.

Even then she'd been too good for him. She was too smart, too studious and too kind. He would have broken her heart. Looking back, he realized he probably had broken her heart. He'd sure broken her trust.

"Stop thinking about the past," she told him as she moved away from her desk and pointed to the door.

"Am I that obvious?"

"You always have been," she said simply. "I'll see you tomorrow."

He walked away, more unsure of himself than he'd ever been in his life. As he turned the corner, he glanced back in time to see her smile soften slightly as she glanced at the photo she held in her hands. A photo that, a moment later, she slid behind a framed certificate on top of her bookcase.

Okay, she had her secrets and he had his. They were even. The thought should have kept him from wondering. He should have been able to walk out the door of the center into the warmth of late spring, believing what he'd told himself—that her story didn't matter.

Except it did matter. A lot. He didn't fully understand why, but he needed to know her secrets. He needed to know what she was hiding from him.

Chapter Two

Avery woke up early the next morning. Early enough to make pancakes for breakfast, to kiss her daughter as she headed out the door to catch the bus. Early enough to go in search of Nan, because for fifteen years, when life got messy or she didn't know how to handle a situation, she'd gone to Nan. Avery knew where to find her foster mother. She would be in her workshop.

Nan Guthrie would turn seventy at the end of July but she had more energy than many people half her age. At least that was Avery's opinion of the woman who had taken her in when Avery had been a lost and wounded fourteen-year-old, fresh in state custody after her stepfather was arrested for intent to distribute drugs, and her mother had slipped out the back door and never returned. Every now and then Avery wondered what had happened to her mother, Jima Hammons. But she hadn't lost sleep over her mother's skipping out. It was what Jima had always done.

Which was why she shouldn't have been surprised eleven years ago when Grayson didn't show up for their date. He'd made such a big deal out of it. That night, eleven years ago, he'd told her the whole world was going to know that he thought she was beautiful and he wanted everyone to know they were dating.

She'd been foolish enough at eighteen to believe him. She'd let her guard down, let him into her life, and he'd left her sitting alone at Tilly's. He'd left town and never returned.

She'd gone to his parents and they'd informed her that she shouldn't have set her sights on someone like Grayson. A girl like her? From the wrong side of the tracks? How ridiculous.

Knowing now that he'd been sent away didn't dissolve the years of hurt. Deep down, she'd expected him to show up, to call, to reappear. He hadn't done any of those things. Even a person in trouble can make phone calls. He could have at least told his parents.

Her foster mother, Nan, had been there to pick up the pieces, just as she'd done when Avery first came to live with her. Nan had been there for a dozen girls over the years. She'd loved them through the hard times. She'd been the one to hold them when they cried. She'd given them reasons to believe in themselves.

Nan was a force of nature. She had never married, claiming she'd loved and lost, and it wasn't in her to make another man feel like he came second. She had supported herself over the years by farming and by making wooden riverboats that sold nationwide.

Avery walked across the dew-dampened grass in the direction of the metal building that had become Nan's workshop when she'd finally outgrown the barn. Vaguely, it registered that it was a beautiful morning in mid-May. The kind of morning she loved, when the birds were singing and a soft mist hovered over the James River in the valley.

As she walked, Nan's collie, Sugar, joined her. The dog was damp from running through the fields and probably swimming in the pond. Avery caught a whiff of something unpleasant.

She frowned at the dog. "You found something to roll in, didn't you?"

Sugar gave a happy woof.

The dog tried to move closer to her side but Avery shooed her away. "I don't think so, Sug."

The whir of a saw echoed from the workshop, slicing into the early-morning silence. Sugar took off in search of more adventures. Avery entered the building, cringing at the loud whine of a saw cutting through wood. Nan, her face distorted by the large, protective goggles she wore, gave her a quick glance and a smile. She finished cutting a section of wood and shut the saw off and pushed the googles to the top of her head.

"Quinn off to school?" Nan asked as she set the saw on a worktable.

"She is."

Nan headed for the coffeepot in the small kitchen she'd built in the corner of the work area. "Would you like some coffee?"

"I've had mine, but thank you."

Nan gave her a sideways look as she stirred sugar into her cup. Avery ignored the questioning look and ran her hand down the sides of the boat. The marine-grade plywood would soon be sealed and painted. Sometimes the boats were merely stained so that the wood grain was visible; others were painted in deep greens or earthy browns. What set Nan's boats apart from others was the craftsmanship. The special woodwork around the top of the boat, the dry storage, the seats. She was a master builder.

"What happened?" Nan sat her cup down on the counter and went back to measuring the wood. She was working on the bottom of the boat. The plywood would be cut so that the front of the boat angled in just slightly. Her silence as she worked was a clear invitation for Avery to talk.

"What do you mean?" Avery asked as she perused the equipment at the side of the room. She knew how to run every bit of it. If she'd wanted to, she could have joined Nan in the business. But it hadn't been her calling.

"You've been cross-eyed and sideways since yesterday. Is there something you need to tell me?"

Nan already knew. It was there in the sharp glint of her pale blue eyes, in the arch of her silvery brow.

"How did you know?"

"Patsy at the café." Nan didn't smile. Her bottom lip was held between her teeth as she got her measurements down and drew the arching line, then went to the opposite side to do the exact same measurements.

It shouldn't have come as a surprise that Nan knew. Half the town probably knew that Grayson Stone was back in Pleasant. All of the good gossip didn't come from the local paper, *The Pleasant Gazette*. The good stuff always came from Tilly's Diner. Tilly was the best cook around and also the biggest source of news and information. Patsy was the worst waitress in town but Nan's best friend.

Avery reminded herself that the entire time she'd been living in Kansas City she had missed this small town and the people she'd known her entire life. She'd grown to miss her small country church, the gossip at Tilly's and the slow-moving tractors on the roads that sometimes held up traffic. She had to remind herself because at moments like this, she wished she were back in Kansas City, hidden in the anonymity of the city.

"What did she say?" Avery asked when Nan looked up from measuring, an expectant look on her face.

"Grayson Stone is back in town to deal with that miserable old coot of a father. You'd think a man who had been a lawyer and a county judge would have a measure of decency."

"Water under the bridge. The here and now are my concern," Avery said as she gave a quick glance at the clock that hung on the wall of the small kitchen. The clock was a 1970s masterpiece, Nan had said. It was brass and looked something like the sun. And yet, nothing like the sun.

"You're going to have to tell him," Nan said with customary patience. "He deserves to know."

"Does he?"

"You know he does. And you also know that secrets fester. Like an untreated infection."

"Thanks for putting it in terms I understand," Avery said drily.

"They get septic and turn…" Nan continued.

"I get the point."

"Eventually, they spread." Nan gave her a wry grin. "They even infect the heart."

"I have to go to work." Avery glanced at the clock a second time. "He'll be there today. He's doing community service."

Nan shoved her pencil behind her ear. "Avery, I've

lived a long time and I've come to realize that God has a way of bringing things about for a reason. It might hurt, but perhaps it has to hurt in order to heal."

"You're right," she conceded.

"I usually am. That's a bonus to living a long time. Go ahead, pull the bandage off. It'll only sting for a bit."

"Proud of yourself, aren't you?" Avery asked and then she kissed her foster mom on the cheek.

"I am, somewhat. Tell him. It will be easier than having him find out on his own. Nothing stays secret in a small town, and the only thing worse than the secret is the pain it's going to cause."

"I don't know..." She knew it would happen. Sooner or later he would find out. After all, this was Pleasant, and gossip spread faster than the chicken pox.

"I'll be praying for you," Nan called out as Avery left. The words were more than a salutation; they were a promise and it mattered.

Avery would need Nan's prayers to get through this day.

Leaving the workshop, she crossed the large expanse of freshly mowed lawn to her car. The grass sparkled with dew and in the distance, fog hung over the river. Fifteen years ago, Nan's farm had been a haven after Avery's nightmare of a childhood. Now it was home. It had made sense to come back here, to Nan and to Pleasant.

Nan's big craftsman home sat on the south side of Pleasant. The fifty acres of rolling farmland and big oak trees had been in Nan's family for over one hundred years. One section of the property was along the river, and from Nan's sprawling back deck you could sit with a cup of coffee and watch the river meander through the valley below.

It was a short drive from the farm to Pleasant, a river town that had seen its heyday years ago, but seemed to be making a comeback as people returned to enjoy water activities like canoeing, camping and fishing. Pleasant had fortunately never lost its charm. The town was a combination of valley and hills. Old Victorian homes sat alongside newer brick homes on narrow paved streets.

The downtown area was a mishmash of buildings. Pleasant Avenue was a quiet little street just off the highway where businesses sat side by side down the one-way street. The century-old brick-fronted buildings had been well-maintained. Tilly's Diner, the Clip Art Beauty Salon, next to it, the barber shop, Bob the Barber. There were several empty buildings, too. Down the street was the Pleasant Grocery and Dry Goods, and next to that, the post office.

Across the street from the row of stores with their brick-and-metal facades was the Grain and Farm, and next to it a garage and tractor repair shop.

Pleasant was the town that time had forgotten. There was an occasional horse tied to a post in front of the Grain and Farm, sometimes a tractor parked in front of Tilly's. In the way of all small towns, everyone knew everyone else. And if you hadn't been born in Pleasant but merely lived there most of your life, you were probably considered a newcomer.

At the end of Pleasant Avenue was Commercial Street. Commercial Street boasted newer buildings. A small strip mall with a sandwich shop, a boutique clothing store and an insurance agent. On the corner was the gas station, and that was where Avery made a right turn to cross the bridge over the river. A few minutes later she pulled into the parking lot of the Pleasant Residential Care, also known as PRC. The facility was located a couple of miles out of town and was surrounded by green fields with a view of rolling hills, grazing cattle and distant tree-covered hills.

Grayson would be there soon, and she needed to prepare.

Yesterday she might have had a breakdown after he left, going to the laundry room and crying for a solid five minutes until she could pull herself together.

That was yesterday. Today was a new day. She pulled on her confidence like a new coat and headed to the front door. As she entered the facility, the staff and residents greeted her with warm smiles.

Laura waved and gave her a questioning look. She was probably worried because yesterday hadn't been a good day.

"Hey, Avery, are we still running away together next week?" Dallas Parson asked from his chair by the nurses' station.

"Maybe not next week, Dallas." She touched his shoulder and he smiled up at her, his crooked grin the sign of the stroke he was still recovering from. "Did you eat breakfast this morning?"

"Always after me to eat my breakfast." He made a face, complete with a wrinkled nose. "That wife of mine keeps at me, too."

"And that, Dallas, is why we can't run away together."

"Because of the wife?" He rolled his eyes a bit. "She's been a ball and chain for fifty years."

"And you love her more than life itself. That's why you have to eat breakfast. We want you to stay strong so you can complete your physical therapy and go home."

He made a completely dramatic sigh. "I suppose you're right. I guess I have a woman that I've trained. Starting over with a younger one would take too much time for an old man like me."

"You're not old," she told him.

"Just seasoned," he finished. He reached for her hand and gave it a squeeze. "Don't let Grayson Stone get under your skin."

Too late. But she smiled.

Grayson's return could unhinge her life. Completely and irreversibly.

She was going to try not to let that happen.

"Where do you think you're going?" Mathias Stone asked from his chair by the window in the living room.

He was pale and weathered, and resembled nothing of his former tall and imposing self. Grayson paused in the doorway and studied the man who had once been a frightening figure of a human being. Now he just looked frightened. As if Grayson was his security.

"I have to do community service, remember?"

"I took care of that." Mathias growled the words. "I'm a judge."

"You *were* a judge. You're retired now and I have to pay for my crimes."

"I sent you away to get you out of this town and away from that woman."

"That woman?" Grayson asked. "Do you mean Avery?"

"That's the one. Go discover her secrets. That's what you're after, isn't it?"

"What secrets?" Grayson moved a little closer to his father and as he did, he saw the way Mathias clamped down on whatever he'd meant to say. His jaw, fleshy and slack, firmed up and he looked away.

Mathias had been stronger, more himself, when Grayson visited his parents in Springfield, the few times he'd returned to Missouri since being sent to California. The last time he'd been home had been for his mother's funeral. Even then, his dad had been tough as nails.

"Go on, I've got to take a nap."

Grayson brushed a hand over his face. "Everyone in this town is keeping her secrets."

"Well, you've got your own, don't you?"

Grayson glanced away, unable to look his father in the eyes. He didn't want to talk about his past. He was only here for a month or two, just long enough to figure out the best way to care for his father. At the end of the summer he would go back to his life in California.

"I don't have secrets," Grayson denied.

"We all do," his father spoke softly. Soft-spoken was not how Grayson would ever describe the man in the wheelchair. Hard. Demanding. Mean. A man who had expected perfection and had been sadly disappointed in his offspring. Grayson and his older sister had never lived up to Mathias Stone's expectations.

June, Grayson's sister, had left home at seventeen. She'd married young, had a son and a daughter. She was happy, married to her preacher husband and living in Oklahoma. Some people were like that, he realized. Some people found their forever loves and lived a happy life. Not that trouble didn't find them from time to time, because life always included hard times. But all in all, they lived a white-picket-fence kind of life.

"It's high time you have your reckoning." Mathias taunted him with the slightest edge of humor to his voice.

"What does that mean?" Grayson asked.

"Not my place to say."

Grayson shook his head, unable to continue the argument. "Your aide just arrived. I'll let her in and then I'll head out."

"I don't need any help."

"Yes, you do," Grayson countered. "When I'm not here, you need help. I can't give you a shower or help you change clothes."

"I don't need either of those things," Mathias argued.

"Yes, you do."

"Yeah, well, don't forget to feed Tony before you leave."

"I won't forget Tony." Grayson smiled his first real smile of the day. His father had named a llama Tony. That was the livestock on the Stone farm. A llama named Tony, a miniature horse named Dolly and a miniature donkey named Jack. The three had come together, a package deal. He thought the animals said a lot about the person Mathias Stone had become in the years since his family deserted him.

Grayson started for the front door.

"Son," his father called out.

"Yes?" Grayson stopped, waited, hoping his father would tell him something. He felt it, deep down felt it, that he needed to be prepared.

"I'm glad you're here."

The words took Grayson by surprise. So did his answer. "So am I."

He left his father in the capable hands of Nina Rose, the home health-care worker. She was a no-nonsense woman, raised on the river. She had a strong back and a big heart, and the judge listened to her.

When Grayson entered the residential facility, he was taken by the friendliness of the staff and the smiles of the residents. As he walked down the hall, an older woman in a wheelchair reached for his hand.

"Did you bring Annie with you?" she asked.

"I'm sorry?" He didn't know how to answer.

She had a toothless smile and gray hair piled up on her head in a bun. Her hand on his was cool, the skin papery but soft. "Annie said she would come today and I thought you would bring her. She said she'd bring the baby to see me."

"I…I…" he stammered. "I'll try again tomorrow."

"No account son-in-law. I knew she should have married that other boy." She released his hand.

He pulled back, unsure of what to say or if he should say anything. A man seated nearby chuckled at him.

"She's a bit confused," the older man said.

"Oh, okay." Grayson studied the man. "You look familiar, sir."

"I should. I was your neighbor for most of your young and misspent youth."

"Dallas Parson?"

"The one and only. If you're looking for Avery, she's down the hall with Margie. The old gal is having dizzy spells again."

"Thank you. Is there…" Grayson paused, unsure. "Do you need anything?"

Dallas laughed. "No, I'm going to be right as rain in a month or so. Don't let them work you too hard. I have a feeling our Avery might use this as revenge."

"I have the same feeling." He was in trouble and didn't know why. That was the story of his life. He started to walk away but then stopped himself. "Dallas, do you know why she feels the need to get revenge?"

Dallas shook his head. "Sorry, son, this is between the two of you. I wish you well but I'm not getting involved."

"I understand," Grayson told the older gentleman. Yet, he didn't understand. It was as if the entire world was speaking in code and he didn't have the key.

Possessing the knowledge that Avery was otherwise occupied, he headed for her office. It wasn't his best moment, sneaking into the closet-size room, peeking around to make sure he wasn't spotted. But he wanted her secrets and if she wasn't going to reveal them, he'd have to find them himself. Had she been married? Was she still married? Did she have a family?

Why would she feel the need to hide her life from him? They were adults. They'd moved on.

He glanced over her desk. The picture was still hidden away from his prying eyes. With cautious steps he moved to the diploma and reached behind it to pull out the framed photograph. Slowly, he turned it and he studied the two faces that peered up at him from behind the glass.

Everyone had their secrets, but this one changed everything.

He shook his head as he studied the photo. Numbness took over and his heart stopped beating for a moment.

He rubbed his chest as he sucked in air, desperately trying to fill his lungs.

"What are you doing in here?" Avery's voice from the door shook him out of his frozen state, and he looked up, meeting her gaze, seeing her fear.

He didn't know what to say to her. Even if he had the words, he didn't know if he could speak at that moment.

"Give me the picture." She reached out to take it from him.

He pulled back, keeping the frame away from her grasp. Her eyes widened as she realized he knew the truth. The color drained from her face. She reached again, her hand trembling as she grasped at the photo he held in his hand.

"Please, Grayson," she said, her voice trembling. "Please give me the picture."

"Give me my daughter," he countered.

"She isn't…"

He cut her off with a shake of his head. He held on to the photo. A photo of Avery and a little girl. A little girl with dark eyes and dark hair, the light catching flecks of auburn. A little girl with his dimples.

"She obviously is, Avery. You kept her from me. Don't make it worse by lying."

"I didn't keep her from you." She paused, swiping at a tear that trickled down her cheek. "You left."

He almost felt sympathetic toward her. Almost. But the little girl in the picture, the one with the dark hair and flashing eyes, was definitely his. He could see it in her smile, in the sassy tilt of her head, in a million little details.

"What's her name?" The question made the ache in his chest double and triple.

"Quinn," she whispered. "Her name is Quinn Anne."

But not Quinn Stone. Quinn Anne Hammons. He knew without a doubt that Avery hadn't given their daughter his last name.

"Is she ten?" he asked, after doing the math.

Avery nodded. "She just turned ten in April."

"Ten years. I have missed knowing her for ten years. I can't even…" He shook his head. "I thought you needed to forgive me. Now I realize that maybe I'm going to have to find a way to forgive you."

"Forgive me? Did you ever, even once, think about calling?"

"Do you think that makes us even? This isn't a game to me, one where we rack up points to see who gets ahead. I have a child I just found out about and I never would have known her if I hadn't come back. Isn't that right?" The enormity of that weighed down on him. He felt angry, sick, heartbroken and some other emotions he couldn't identify.

Avery didn't respond. She just stood there, pale, sad, beautiful and guilty as charged.

"I want to meet her," he said as he took a step closer to the woman who had betrayed him. *Betrayed* was a strong word. But his feelings at the moment were pretty strong. He couldn't do anything other than be angry with her.

Another tear trickled down her cheek. This one traced a path to her chin and dripped off without her catching it. "I don't know how to do this."

"Because you never considered that at some point, someday, I might show up? Or because you never thought about searching for me? The internet is an amazing thing."

She shook her head as more tears raced down her face. He reached past her and closed the office door.

"I should have tried harder."

He agreed with that. "Yes, you should have."

"You make my life complicated, Grayson," she said. "We were never ever going to be right for each other. We came from different worlds, you and me. I was never in your life, not really. I never fit in your circle. I was your little secret, not good enough for you to bring me around your friends or even to be seen with in public."

The words stunned him. Had he really been that person?

"We're no longer those two kids, Avery. None of that matters now. What matters is today."

"You think it will be that simple?" she asked, her voice breaking.

"No, it won't be simple, but I will be in my daughter's life," he assured her. "Either you choose a way to handle this or I'll do it for you."

"I'll figure it out."

"Good choice."

He opened the door and walked out of her office, reeling with the knowledge that he had a daughter. While he'd been living his life in California, she'd been living hers here in Pleasant. And he hadn't known.

He should have called Avery. He'd known it eleven years ago and he knew it now. He'd let his parents make decisions for him because his life had been spiraling out of control and he'd run out of options.

None of that mattered now. What mattered was a girl named Quinn. His daughter. That connected him to Avery in a way he never would have imagined.

He left the facility and walked to his truck. As he

got behind the wheel, he saw that Avery had followed him to the door. She stood on the other side of the glass, the barrier making her image waver and fade in and out of focus.

The girl he'd known all of those years ago was gone, and in her place was a woman, a mother who knew herself and how to be strong. He realized he'd never truly known her. She'd always been in his life, a little girl with dirty clothes and bruises on her arms. As a teenager she'd gone from a towheaded blond with freckles and dirt smudges on her cheek to a beauty who was overlooked because she grew up in the wrong area of town. She'd worn hand-me-down clothes, studied furiously and ignored the taunts of the kids who had assumed they were her betters.

He hadn't overlooked her. He'd just underestimated her. He'd hurt her. Truth be told, he'd played games with her, with her heart, with her life. He'd been selfish. He'd done everything wrong and not much right.

Now that girl was the mother of his child.

Chapter Three

"Are you okay?" Laura stepped into her office, not bothering to knock. Or maybe she had knocked and Avery hadn't heard. She'd been numb since she discovered Grayson in her office.

How was it possible to be so numb and yet feel the worst emotional pain of her life? And that didn't include her mind, which was going in circles trying to decide on a plan of action. Her life had been carefully balanced and now it was like a child's top, spinning out of control.

"I'm good," Avery assured her friend. She added a stiff and probably unconvincing smile to punctuate the statement.

"Right." Laura drawled the word out, then she pushed the door closed. "Talk. We have five minutes while the aides help residents back to their rooms."

"What am I supposed to say in five minutes?"

"Mr. All Hat was back today and he didn't stay for his community service."

"So?"

"We could start with him. He's obviously someone important to you."

"He isn't important to me." Her gaze strayed to the picture of herself and Quinn.

Laura's gaze followed hers and then she stepped around the desk and reached for the photo. Her eyes widened and she whistled. "Whoa, I didn't notice that yesterday. I was too busy getting an eyeful of a handsome stranger. Even a happily engaged woman like myself can see that he's pretty gorgeous."

Avery took the photo from Laura, her eyes watering as she stared down at the image of her smiling, sassy daughter. "It's that obvious?"

"You know it is. She has his eyes, his dimples, even that stubborn chin of hers now makes sense. Oh, Avery, I can't even imagine how you must be feeling right now."

"Ashamed. Afraid. Panicked. Do I need to go on?"

"No, I think you should stop before you send yourself straight over the edge of the cliff you're standing on."

"The cliff looks so appealing right about now," she said as she took a deep, shuddery breath and set the photo back on her desk. "I have to do something. I have to find a way to tell my daughter that she has a dad and he is in town."

"She's a smart girl. She's always known she has a dad. The *in town* part might be the shocker, though. Why don't you go home? Take a sick day."

"I'm not sure how a sick day would help."

"You've got this, Avery. And you're not alone. You have friends. You have Nan. And you have faith. God is never surprised. The situations we encounter might knock us off our feet, but they don't knock Him off His feet. Pray."

"Thank you. And yes, I'll see if I can leave early."

"If you need me…"

Avery rarely hugged anyone, but she grabbed her friend in a quick embrace. "I'm glad God sent you to Pleasant."

In twenty-nine years on this earth, she'd never had a friend like Laura Anderson.

Even her many foster sisters hadn't been her closest friends. Maybe because as teens they'd all been wounded, angry and fighting to survive. They hadn't been able to really bond because they'd been too immersed in survival mode.

"Go. We'll all still be here tomorrow."

Fifteen minutes later Avery hit the road. As she drove, she rolled the car windows down and played worship music. She didn't go right home. She drove down Pleasant Avenue, turned left on Riverside Drive and followed the narrow, paved road a mile out of town to the run-down trailer park where she'd grown up. The trailer she'd lived in now had missing siding. The roof had been patched with pieces of sheet metal. The porch was gone.

Nothing remained but memories.

Memories of being forgotten. Memories of being ridiculed.

Memories of a girl who used to dream of the day she'd return and show them all that they weren't better than she was. She had few positive memories of this place, this town. And yet, she'd returned. She'd returned to Pleasant, to the church she'd grown up in, the same church where those same girls who had ridiculed her on the school playground had pretended to be her friends in Sunday school.

Many of those girls still attended the Pleasant First

Community Church. They were adults now. With crying toddlers, baby food stains on their best dresses, and diaper bags instead of designer purses. Somehow, growing up had evened the playing field, and she found she even liked some of the same people who had made her childhood so miserable.

She'd forgiven them because it made more sense than the bitterness she'd harbored for so many years. Staying angry took too much energy.

It was all water under the bridge, except for Quinn. And Grayson.

She sat for a long time, staring at the run-down trailer, trying to picture her mother's face. She'd had blond hair and sunken-in cheeks. She had never truly laughed, not with humor. Her laughter had often been the product of a drug-induced high. Tears had been more the norm.

The one thing that Avery could guarantee was that Quinn would never ever know that kind of life.

Every single decision Avery made, she made with Quinn in mind. Quinn would never feel abandoned, hurt or forgotten, not by Avery. And Avery was adamant that she'd do everything in her power to make sure Grayson didn't hurt their daughter.

She needed to make sure Grayson understood he couldn't take her daughter. The thought of losing Quinn to Grayson might have been buried deep inside her for ten years, since Quinn's birth. She'd ignored it, pretended it wasn't a driving factor in her life, but it had always been there.

She pulled out of the driveway without looking back. With an hour to spare before school got out, she drove to the property she had bought to build a house on. The five acres sat a little too close to the Stone farm, a fact that hadn't bothered her when she'd thought the Stones resided in Springfield and when she'd thought Grayson would never set foot in Pleasant ever again.

But then the judge had returned to town. And now, Grayson.

This property was her future, though. It was a part of her dream, to turn this place of rolling hills, big oaks and the occasional dogwood into a home for herself and Quinn. She had planned the house herself, brick and natural wood, big windows and wide, covered porches. They would be settled here with good neighbors, a church family that loved them and a future that was secure.

She didn't want to let go of that dream. She wouldn't let it be one more thing for Grayson to take from her.

She parked in the gravel next to the framed house, just a concrete foundation and the skeleton of what would be their home. A home that was meant to shelter them, protect them, make them feel safe.

All of her life this had been her goal. Her short time at Nan's had taught her to believe in the impossible, to set goals, to trust God for her future. Those were things Grayson couldn't take. And he hadn't stolen everything. He hadn't known it, but he'd given her the best part of her life, Quinn.

She walked through the home that had no walls. In her mind she could see it all clearly. The living room where they would set up a Christmas tree. The kitchen where they would bake cookies. The dining room and small sitting room with a view of distant hills.

She could see her daughter growing up here. But now the dream had changed. Grayson had returned and he would somehow have to be involved in their lives. Her throat closed at the thought of Christmases without Quinn. Holidays Quinn would be in California with Grayson, and she'd be all alone.

Just then a car door slammed. She walked back through the house to see who had arrived. Her heart sank at the sight of the man standing next to his truck. Grayson, a cowboy hat pushed back on his head as he studied the house. Then his gaze landed on her.

Her heart stuttered, caught somewhere between past and present. Grayson the dream, the enemy, the father of her daughter. Having him here made it all too real. He was going to be a part of her present and her future. He was no longer just a person from her past. Not that he had ever really been the past. Quinn had kept him a real figure in her life.

If only her heart didn't quake a little at the sight of him. Traitorous heart, it had always reacted to him in just this way, even after he'd hurt her. Even knowing the things he'd said about her. Even now her heart wished he could have been the person she imagined him to be instead of the one who had hurt her and left her.

Her heart might not understand the need for distance, but she did. She would never let him hurt her again. She wouldn't let him hurt Quinn. And that meant if he took one step into her daughter's life, *his* daughter's life, she wouldn't let him walk away.

As much as Grayson's being in her life frightened her, the idea of him hurting Quinn frightened her more. She could protect herself. She could handle his rejection. Quinn was only a child and didn't have the coping skills to handle the hurt he might cause.

"I was in town and heard you'd bought this piece of

land," he said as he crossed the uneven ground to the building site. "This is going to be nice."

He studied the site of her future home and she studied him. She tried to decide the best way forward with a man she'd learned she couldn't trust. Yet somehow, he always lured her in. It was more than his country-boy good looks. As a grown man, he'd put a polish to those teen looks of his, and that was something she couldn't deny. But there was more to him than that. There was a sincerity in his eyes that always drew her.

She desperately wanted to trust him. That was what had always landed her in trouble—trusting Grayson.

"Avery?" he asked, drawing her back to the present.

"Thank you. It's been my dream for a long time, to have a house on this piece of land. When it came up for sale, I bought it."

"I remember," he said, surprising her.

"What?"

He came nearer, pulling off his cowboy hat as he continued to study the building. "I remember you talking about this piece of land. If I remember correctly, it was the dogwood trees and the pond that you loved."

Avery's cheeks pinkened. He had remembered their picnic at the pond. It had been spring and the dogwoods and redbuds had been vibrant purple and white against the backdrop of emerald green grass. That he recalled the day shouldn't mean anything to her. She should know better than to be affected by it, but she was.

The memory of that afternoon came back to her, so clearly she could almost see it. They'd been driving back roads, the windows rolled down and the early-spring air whipping through his car. The radio had played a pop love song from decades past, with the melancholy lyrics that begged to know what love is. Back then she'd been living that emotional song that seemed to cater to the hearts of lonely teen girls. Every time she'd heard it, she'd swooned and thought of Grayson and her. She'd thought he might be the one to show her love.

Instead he'd only shown her more of the heartache and pain that came with loving someone who didn't really love her back.

He was no longer her dream. She no longer needed his love or the heartache he promised to be a whole person. What she truly needed was security and a place to build a life for her daughter.

This place. This piece of land that remained a promise, a dream, unchanging. Solid.

He walked away from her, wandering through the wall-less rooms, examining the frame of her future home. She started to tell him she hadn't invited him in but she stopped herself when he tossed her a look.

"I'm not going to take your daughter, you know," he said. "*Our* daughter. But I do want to know her. I do want to be a part of her life."

"I see."

"I want to help you raise her. If this is the home you want for our daughter," he said, "I want to help you build this house. If you don't want me to build it, at least let me help pay for it."

"I'll pay for my own house, thank you very much."

"I owe you ten years of child support."

"You owe me nothing, Grayson."

He stepped away from her, his dark eyes taking on the hint of mossy green she remembered so well. "I know you don't trust me, but we're going to have to work through that."

She didn't like being told what to do.

He put a hand on a two-by-four that would be part of her living room wall. "Who's building this house for you?" he asked.

"A contractor out of Branson."

He studied the frame and shook his head. "Why did you pick him?"

"I don't think you have the right to question me," she said, hearing her voice get all defensive and knowing his would, too.

"I'm not getting in your business, Avery. But building is my business and I'm concerned. I can already see he's cutting corners."

"He's just trying to save me money," she defended. But now the doubts began to pile up. He was so good at causing her to doubt herself.

"Cutting corners is saving him money, not you."

She studied the frame of the house with new eyes, trying to see what he saw. She didn't see anything, but she accepted that he knew far more than she would about building homes. "I'll talk to him about it."

"If you need help…" He left the offer open and she nodded. It didn't hurt, accepting his help. Not the way she thought it might.

In the distance she heard a school bus. She glanced at her watch. "I have to go. Quinn will be home soon."

"I'd like to meet her."

"Let me talk to her first."

As she walked to her car, she saw the yellow bus top a hill, then slow to a stop, red lights blinking. It was stopping at Grayson's father's place.

"Why is the bus stopping at your dad's?" she asked. But the question didn't need to be asked. She already knew.

From the look on Grayson's face, he knew, as well. They were about to confront their daughter as parents.

She closed her eyes and prayed that she would be strong, that Grayson wouldn't break their hearts and that Quinn would forgive her.

That wasn't too much to ask, was it?

Grayson stood next to Avery, and it wasn't really his life flashing before his eyes but the present and the future coming together. The woman he'd hurt. The bus, lights flashing, stopping a short distance away.

Across the ten acres of pasture that stood between his dad's place and Avery's, he could see a small figure exiting the bus. From that distance he couldn't make out anything about her, but from Avery's reaction, he knew it was his daughter. He watched as she headed toward his father's house.

"I have to get to her," Avery said with a noticeable panic in her voice.

"Get in my truck. We can go together."

"I'll take my car," she said as she hurried away from him.

"Of course." He let her go, and for some reason he couldn't make himself hurry to his truck. His feet dragged and his thoughts circled around the small figure he'd seen from a distance. His daughter.

Would she like him? Would she have the same resentment her mother had for him? He'd only seen a photograph and he already loved her, so much so that it ached deep in his heart. He wondered if that was natural.

If he'd seen her as an infant, would he have felt that immediate connection to the dark-haired, dark-eyed girl who was his child?

In only a few minutes he would know.

He pulled up to the farmhouse that his dad had insisted on returning to. Avery had already arrived. His dad was on the porch and Nina was with him. Quinn, small but mighty, was poised on the steps as if preparing to run.

Avery was out of her car and running to Quinn's side. Grayson got out of his truck and followed, moving slower, giving them time. Then his gaze connected with his daughter's. Quinn. He had a daughter named Quinn. She looked like him. And at that moment her round eyes were filled with anger, wonder and all sorts of emotions that she had every right to.

Everything was in slow motion as he waited. She stood there, just a kid in skinny jeans and a long T-shirt, her head held high as she stared him down. She was tall and awkward; she was brave but uncertain. Yes, he had been correct in knowing he would love her immediately. She was his.

"Quinn," Avery began, but at the look of rage in their daughter's eyes, she stopped speaking.

"I heard them talking at recess. Mrs. Jackson, the substitute, was telling Fanny Maxwell, the cook, that she'd seen Grayson Stone and that 'it wouldn't be long before everyone knew who poor Quinn Hammons's daddy is.'"

"I'm so sorry," Avery said in a hushed voice. She reached for her daughter but Quinn shook her head.

She turned to look at him again. "Are you my dad?" Quinn asked, ignoring her mother. Quinn bit down on her bottom lip, her mossy-brown eyes continuing to study him. "Well?"

Right, he hadn't answered her question. He looked to Avery because he didn't know what to say. As much as he wanted to claim this girl, he didn't want to move too quickly. He didn't want to hurt her mother. Avery gave a reluctant nod.

"I am," he answered. It was either the most profound words he'd ever uttered or the most inept. This slip of a girl confronting him with a mixture of bravado and fear was his daughter.

Quinn jerked around to face Avery. "Were you ever going to tell me?"

"Yes, I was going to tell you." Avery's voice was broken, devastated, but she didn't cry.

Quinn started to shove past him, to escape. Avery reached for her arm. "Quinn, wait…"

"No," Quinn said, her eyes drowning in tears. She looked at them all. Her mother, Grayson, the judge and his caregiver. She looked angry and frightened. She appeared desperate to escape.

"Give her a minute," Grayson said as he reached for Avery's arm, stopping her pursuit of their daughter. Their eyes met and hers were pretty intense. He pulled back, but watched her take a deep breath and briefly close her eyes.

This had thrown them all into a tailspin, even Avery, who had been the keeper of her secrets.

"I need to explain." Avery shook free from his hand. "I'm not sure what to tell her or how to explain but I can't let her just walk away like this."

"I think she needs a few seconds to think and process

everything." He kept his voice low, wishing his father, the judge, wasn't a witness.

"You're the parenting expert now?" Avery replied as she moved to the steps. She did not keep her tone low.

"No, I'm not. I just know that sometimes a person needs time alone to breathe."

"Let's all just take a minute," Grayson's dad chimed in. He'd remained unusually quiet throughout the drama. He moved closer now, with Nina helping him on his walker.

He took a seat on an old bench. His speech was still halting and he hadn't regained full use of his left side.

Avery took a few deep breaths. "I only wanted to give my daughter stability. Now, instead, I've given her a father who will be in and out of her life. A father who couldn't even call me to let me know he was leaving town."

What she really meant to say, he guessed, was that if she couldn't trust him, how could she trust him with their daughter? She had a valid point.

"I'm sorry," he said. "I know this isn't what you wanted but it's what we have. I'm going to be in my daughter's life."

"Part-time," she said with a sadness in her green eyes that derailed any objections he might have had to her words.

She stared after Quinn. The girl had walked a good distance from the house, his dad's old basset hound at her side. She plopped herself down in the grass and the dog, only a foot tall but three feet long, crawled onto her lap.

A hint of a smile curved Avery's lips. Her hair had come loose from the bun that had held it in place that morning. The pale pink scrubs with kittens she wore were adorable. She was a beautiful woman who had kept him from his child.

From that truth, resentment grew.

"This is new territory for both of us," he offered, working really hard to be patient and to remember she had a lot of reasons to not trust him. He'd had to learn to trust himself, so it made sense.

"Stop trying to placate me." Her voice was an edgy whisper.

"You'll need to work out custody and child support," Grayson's dad said, ever the judge.

"Not now, Dad."

"I don't want child support. I don't need it," Avery insisted. "And Mathias Stone, you do not have a right to give advice. You're part of the reason we're in this situation."

"What does *that* mean?" Grayson asked as he looked from Avery to his father.

"Ask him," Avery said.

"I will, but I'll do it later."

Avery walked down the steps to the yard. "Fine. For the record, we will work it out. For Quinn's sake, we need to figure out the co-parenting thing. That's all I want from you, Grayson. I don't want you involved in my life. I don't want your money. But I want you to always be honest with our daughter. She may act mature, but she's only ten and she is probably going to think that you're going to stay here. We both know that isn't the case. You have a life and a career in California, not Missouri."

"You're right," he said. "I agree to your terms as long as you agree to let me spend time with Quinn."

He wanted to promise that he wouldn't break either of their hearts but now wasn't the time. He hadn't earned the right to give her those reassurances.

A part of him feared he couldn't live up to her expectations. What-ifs were a big part of his life, and he knew he was always one slipup from letting himself down and hurting the people who cared about him.

"We need to talk to her," Avery said, glancing back at him as she headed for Quinn.

An invitation to go with her. He would take that as a promising step forward. He followed her across the yard in the direction of their daughter.

Their daughter. The word unsettled him as he thought of the totality of that word. They had a child. He and Avery. At that moment their daughter sat beneath the shade of an old willow tree, the basset hound curled up next to her. She was pulling up clover and picking the flowers apart. Or maybe making a chain? He watched, awed by the realization that this child was his.

He wanted to know everything about her.

"You're going to frighten her," Avery said softly, and it took him a moment to realize she was speaking to him.

"I'm sorry?"

"The look on your face. I don't know what that look is, Grayson, but it's so happy and fierce that it's almost frightening." Her expression softened and the corner of her mouth lifted the tiniest bit. It was a chink in her armor and it gave him hope. She had things against him, real things, not made up. He'd hurt her. But maybe, just maybe, they could be friends.

Or at least not enemies.

* * *

Quinn looked up from the flower chain she was making, a foot-long strand of white clover. She pushed to her feet and waited for them.

"Okay, let's do this," Quinn said as they joined her under the willow tree.

Grayson looked to Avery, needing her to lead him in this conversation. She was the parent. He was the man who'd joined the game about ten years too late. And yet, for some reason, Avery seemed to be the one struggling to find words. She drew in a deep, tremulous breath and briefly closed her eyes before speaking.

"Quinn, this is your father, Grayson Stone. I should have told you about him." Avery gave him a quick look as she made the introductions. "I should have told him about you. You both deserved better from me."

"It would have been better than hearing it from strangers." Quinn scrunched her face and blinked away tears.

"Oh, Quinn." Avery gathered her in her arms and held her tight. "I'm so sorry. I thought I was protecting you."

"It's okay, Mom." Quinn mumbled into Avery's shoulder. "But I can't breathe."

"I should have told you," Avery said as she released Quinn. "I'm sorry."

Quinn shrugged and swiped at her eyes.

"I figured if you wanted to talk about it, you would have said something." Quinn's attention turned to Grayson. "Now what do we do? I mean, you're here but I don't know why."

Grayson cleared his throat. "I came to take care of my father. I have to make arrangements for his care."

"So you're going to stay here and take care of your dad?" Quinn asked.

His confidence seemed to falter, but he'd promised honesty to her. "No, I can't stay."

"Oh," Quinn responded as she slid her hand into Avery's. Avery was reassured by the gesture. Her daughter reaching for her meant they were still a team.

"I know this is tough, but I'm going to find a way to make things up to you," he assured their daughter. "We'll figure this out, me and your mom."

The two of them, as a team. Avery swallowed a few choice things she would have liked to say to him. She fought back the worry, that her relationship with her daughter would change. She'd survived so many things in her life, and this wasn't the worst thing to ever happen. And for Quinn, maybe this was meant to be.

"What about me?" Quinn asked. "Won't I have a say?"

"Of course," Grayson assured her. "Whatever it takes, we'll make this work."

"I guess you're going to have to buy me a horse," Quinn said. Her tone took on a watery quality, the sound of tears about to fall, but she smiled.

"Quinn!" Avery shook her head. A horse? They couldn't have a horse.

"A horse isn't too much to ask for," he agreed.

"I didn't agree to a horse," Avery told him. He grinned at her objection and she wondered if this was the new normal for herself and her daughter. Would he forever be between them, the good one, making dreams come true while Avery had to be the parent who maintained discipline?

"So you don't have a family somewhere, do you?

A wife, a few kids?" Quinn visibly pulled the rug out from under him with the shift in conversation. It was a question Avery hadn't thought to ask so maybe Quinn had shocked them both.

"No wife and no kids," he answered.

"Just me," Quinn responded.

"Yes, just you." Grayson smiled at the statement.

Avery could have told him that was the wrong choice of words. Quinn gave him a look that caused him to clear his throat and try again. "I'm glad you're in my life, Quinn."

"For however long it takes you to settle things with your dad. My grandfather." She wrinkled her nose. "Wow. I have a grandfather. And a dad. But what happens in two months? I mean, will we get to visit or something? Christmas here, spring break there?"

"We'll work it all out," he promised. Avery wanted to tell him he didn't have a right to make promises. If they were going to work this parenting business out as a team, then he didn't get to promise things like horses, visits and Christmas together. Not without her approval, or at least seeking her opinion.

"Quinn, this is new territory for all of us," Avery started, then she didn't know what else to say. Grayson waited, his expression gentle, as if he understood. "I know that we will work out visits and…"

She couldn't get the words out. She felt a lump of fear as she thought about trusting her daughter with Grayson, a man she resented, who she didn't trust. A man who had walked away without a backward glance. But what if she was wrong about that? And about him.

Before she could commit to those visits, she had to

know that she could trust her daughter with him. She had to know the man and separate him from the teenager who had broken her heart.

Chapter Four

Grayson got up early on Saturday morning and headed to the barn on his father's farm. He hadn't slept much the past few nights, not since the meeting with Quinn. Avery had said that they could spend Saturday evening together. He hadn't quite figured out if she meant the three of them or just Grayson and Quinn.

"You're up early," Mathias grumbled as Grayson headed into the kitchen to pour himself a cup of too-strong coffee, the kind his dad bought from an online bulk distributor. It wasn't good, just cheap.

"There's work to do on this place if you're going to insist on staying here." Grayson spooned too much sugar into the coffee. "Do you want a cup?"

"I've been up for an hour. I've already had mine."

"Why do you get up so early?" Grayson asked as he sat down at the table across from his father.

Mathias scrubbed a hand across his grizzly cheek. "I don't sleep much these days. Too much going on in here."

His dad pointed to his head with a trembling hand. Mathias's speech had improved in the past month or so, making it easier to understand his words. From time to time he slurred or dropped a sound, but he was getting better every day.

"I can imagine," Grayson sympathized. He'd long ago stopped hating his father. Mathias had been cold and a hard taskmaster. That had been the only way he knew how to parent.

"I bought her that land, you know," Mathias told him.

"I don't think you did," Grayson said, sure he was confused.

"I heard she was interested and I knew she couldn't afford it. I told Wilson, the owner of that piece of property to cut the price and I'd pay the difference."

His brow furrowed, Grayson just nodded. "She wouldn't be happy if she knew."

"She's got mettle, that girl," Mathias complimented. "Always did."

"And yet, you acted as if she was never good enough."

"I did what I thought was right. At the time it seemed right. Now…" The judge turned a shade of red that indicated he was embarrassed. "I never meant to hurt her. Or you."

Grayson took another swig of coffee and got up to pour the rest of the bitter brew down the drain. "I don't want to discuss this."

"I knew."

"You what?" Grayson slammed his cup down hard and dark liquid sloshed over the side.

"She came to us, told us about the baby. We didn't believe her. I'm sorry."

"You're sorry? You kept me from my daughter for ten years and you're sorry? I missed out on most of my daughter's childhood, Dad. I'm not sure if she'll ever forgive me, or Avery, for that."

"Give it time," Mathias said with a tremor in his voice.

"Don't give me advice." Grayson instantly forgot all of the warm feelings he'd been having for his father.

He left the house, the ancient basset hound trotting after him. As he crossed the lawn, he heard a bray and changed course. The miniature donkey was out again and the miniature horse was right behind him, squeezing herself through the barbed-wire fence. The barn, the fence, all of it was in need of repair. The place had been left in the care of an old drunk who had done his best, which wasn't near good enough. And now Grayson's dad wanted to live here again. He shook his head.

Grayson paused midstride and brushed a hand through his hair. There were moments like this one, this week, that he really needed a meeting. He needed people like himself, who understood addiction and understood just how difficult it was to not use drugs, to not drink while facing a crisis.

Being in Missouri near his old stomping grounds, and knowing that old friends and enablers were easy to find, reminded him that his sobriety, even nine years' worth, could be broken in a single moment.

He'd avoided this town for that very reason, because avoiding Pleasant meant avoiding the temptations of a life he'd overcome.

He glanced heavenward. "We've got this," he said to the only higher power he believed in. "I know You're here and I know You are my strength, my very real help in times of trouble."

When no one else was there, God was there. He

could do this. He knew he could because he'd lived through tougher times than this. The loss of his mother and then his uncle Edward had tested him, shaken him to the core.

The miniature donkey named Jack and the miniature horse named Dolly were now trotting around the yard, flaunting their freedom to Grayson and Tony the llama who ran up and down the fence line, looking for his own way out.

"Back inside, you two pests." He cut the pair off, sliding on the dew-dampened grass as he did.

Jack ran left and Dolly pushed between Grayson and the fence. The basset hound, Fred, ran in circles, barking at all of them.

"I'm a professional contractor with a degree in architecture," he yelled at the pair. "I'm not a miniature livestock wrangler."

From the old farmhouse's back porch, laughter drifted across the lawn. His father's laughter.

"I didn't sign on for this," Grayson yelled.

"It builds character," his dad shouted.

The rumble of an engine and the rattle of a livestock trailer stopped his pursuit of the miscreant livestock. He watched as a truck pulled around and then backed the trailer toward a gate.

"What now?" he grumbled, knowing his father couldn't hear and wouldn't answer even if he could.

The driver's door of the truck opened and Tucker Church climbed out. Grayson hadn't seen the man in years. The changes took him by surprise. Tall, spindly Tucker Church, the guy with glasses, wild curls and a penchant for science had been a good friend but the two hadn't run in the same social circles.

Tucker had been a good kid. But the girls hadn't been interested much in Tucker. He'd been too serious and too scrawny. He was no longer scrawny and he had a few inches on Grayson's six feet.

"Tucker, good to see you." Grayson held out a hand to the other man.

Tucker took his hand in a brief and rather bone-crushing grip. "Been a few years."

"Yeah, it has." Grayson flexed his fingers and glanced at the stock trailer full of cattle. "What's this?"

"Cattle."

"I know what they are. Why are you here with a load of cattle?"

Tucker chuckled, his gray eyes twinkling with mirth. "I guess they're a gift for you. Your dad called me up and said you need something to keep you busy while you're here. I think he's hoping this will convince you to stay."

"Before you unload the cattle, I need to talk to the judge. I'm not here to manage his livestock and there's no way he can do it himself. I also don't know if these fences will hold a kitten, let alone cattle."

Tucker shot a look over Grayson's shoulder. "I'd say your theory about the fences is correct. Dolly and Jack are on the loose again."

"I know they are. It's becoming a habit of theirs. And since you're the one who helped him haul those three from the livestock auction, you can help me put them in."

"Right, I wish I could but I have to get home to my niece. I'll help you unload this bunch and the other two are on you."

"I thought we were friends?" Grayson said as Tucker unlatched the back of the trailer.

"Friends?" Tucker paused, giving him a hard stare. "Friends usually talk to each other more than once a decade. Friendship might mean more to some of us than it does to others."

Grayson stood there silent as Tucker opened the gate, moved the back door of the trailer and started to unload a dozen angus heifers. Character-building his foot.

He glanced around, looking for Dolly and Jack. Dolly had found a patch of clover near the house. Jack was nowhere in sight.

"Hey, man, I owe you an apology," Grayson acknowledged.

"You don't owe me anything," Tucker said. "But I'm going to warn you. Don't hurt Avery and Quinn. I'd take it personally if you played with her emotions and then walked away. Again."

"I'm not here to hurt Avery."

Tucker arched a dark brow. "Quinn is a good kid, Grayson. She's remarkable."

"You seem like you know Avery and Quinn pretty well. Is there something between you and Avery?" As the words tumbled out, Grayson felt like a jealous teenager.

Tucker's mouth hitched up at the corner. "Nah, I'm just a friend. But I'm a loyal friend."

The way Tucker said it, the insinuation was pretty obvious. Tucker didn't think Grayson was loyal. Maybe he hadn't been, but he'd had eleven years to change, to become a better person. Not that he could tell Tucker that. Words weren't going to mean much to the people in Pleasant, to the people he'd hurt.

The cattle Tucker had unloaded trotted not too far into the field and started grazing. Across the way Grayson could see the outline of a house frame. Avery's house.

"I want a relationship with my daughter," he told Tucker. "And I guess I want to protect Avery from a contractor that is probably taking her to the cleaners."

"That's it?"

"Yeah, that's it." He drew in a breath and decided to confide in a man whom he used to call friend. "Tucker, I'm an addict. I've been clean for nine years. I'd like to say I'm proud of that, but I'm wise enough to know that pride can be tricky. Pride can make a man think he can't fall. These past few days have taught me that I'm still pretty fallible."

"Are you okay?" Tucker asked with a sense of ease that Grayson envied.

"I'm good, just realizing for the first time in a long time that an addict is only one moment away from slipping."

"If I can help…" Tucker offered.

"Thanks, I appreciate that." He swallowed a lot of regret, and his pride along with it. "You're right, I wasn't a very good friend. I hope you'll forgive me."

"Don't apologize to me. I didn't like you that much anyway," he said with dry mirth that took Grayson by surprise.

"Is that why you agreed to the three amigos and the herd of cattle?" Grayson asked. "Trying to get back at me?"

"I think maybe your dad is hoping they'll keep you busy. Maybe he understands more than you realize."

"I didn't come home to be a cattle farmer."

"Too busy in California being the big-time contractor?"

"I slid into that position."

Grayson turned on a spigot over the water trough. As water poured in, he turned to search for Dolly and Jack. The llama was still pacing inside the fence. Dolly had moved closer but still grazed.

"I'll help you get her in," Tucker offered.

"Help me find Jack?" Grayson asked.

"Nah, that one is your problem. I have the veterinarian on his way to my house to work cattle and I can't leave Shay alone."

"Shay?"

"My niece. She's Jana's daughter. My sister and her husband are having marital problems and both are a bit too busy to be parents. They sent Shay to live with me."

Grayson was surprised by the path Tucker's life had taken. "Remember when the life we wanted consisted of being river rats, and maybe building some cabins to rent or taking people fishing?"

"I did that, too," Tucker said with a straight face. "I built the cabins and I have a canoe and kayak business on the old campground my uncle owned."

He shouldn't have been surprised. Tucker had always been the one planning his life, and that life had always been in his hometown. Grayson thought back to their teen years and realized he hadn't planned much, other than fun and mischief.

In hindsight, the good times hadn't really been so good. He had holes in his memory, holes in his relationships and a daughter he barely knew.

All those good times had landed him in rehab and

in numerous AA meetings, trying to stay clean and on track. He was blessed that his God was bigger than his mischief making and fortunately he'd survived.

"Trips down memory lane can be hard," Tucker said, his tone and expression conveying his understanding.

"Yeah, they can be. Maybe my dad is right. Cattle might be exactly what I need. The three amigos that won't stay in these fences, not so much."

"Paul had a thorn in his side. Tony, Jack and Dolly might be yours. Maybe those three are teaching you something," Tucker said with a grin.

"And what would that lesson be?"

"You'll figure it out," Tucker said. From the glimmer of amusement in his eyes, he was enjoying this way too much. "Call me sometime and we'll go fishing."

"I will."

With that, Tucker headed for his truck.

"Hey," Grayson called out. "Aren't you going to help me get these animals in?"

Tucker laughed. "That wouldn't be any fun. I wouldn't want to keep you from learning whatever lesson those three are teaching you. And here's hoping you find Jack. He's long gone. If it helps, he likes to stroll through Pleasant on occasion. That might be why the former owners sold him."

As he chased Dolly in the direction of the barn, Grayson got the feeling that this wasn't about a lesson. This was more about Tucker paying him back for the pain he'd caused others.

Most of all, the pain he'd caused Avery. He could have told the other man that he didn't need any help feeling sorry or guilty. Three animals didn't need to take him down a notch, the look in Avery's eyes when she'd introduced him to his daughter had already done so.

He had a lot to make up for and not a lot of time in which to do it.

Saturday mornings in Pleasant meant Tilly's Diner for breakfast, then Bible study for the ladies of Pleasant Community Church and anyone else who wanted to join. Except men; they knew better than to join in.

When her work schedule allowed, Avery joined the ladies for Bible study. Quinn enjoyed it because Tilly would invite her into the kitchen or let her help clear tables and do dishes in exchange for dessert or ice cream. If Tilly was baking, Quinn was at her side, being her sous-chef, cutting and measuring and chopping.

Tilly had given Avery much the same treatment as a child that she gave Quinn now. If she'd seen Avery wandering by herself, ten years old and nowhere to go, she would invite her in and let her bus tables for tips. For that reason, Tilly said she got the role of honorary great aunt.

Avery felt secure in the knowledge that her daughter had the love of people in their community. She might be a single parent, but she had a huge support system.

This Saturday in May had Avery questioning if living in a small town really was the best thing for herself and her daughter. Patsy, Nan, Betsy, Flora, Amy and Franny were all gathered at the table, their Bibles opened to Ephesians Chapter Four.

Betsy read verses about not allowing the sun to go down on one's anger. She cleared her throat as she continued on to the end of the chapter, her voice rising a notch as she said to be kind to one another, tenderhearted, forgiving one another. She looked up and then dropped her gaze to her Bible and finished the verse.

Flora let out a hushed, "Oh my."

Franny Lawson said, "Hmmm."

Avery closed her Bible with a resounding thump. "Stop, y'all. I am not angry and I don't need to forgive him."

Nan snickered, and Nan was not a woman given to such a thing.

"I mean it," Avery said. "If you all have something to say, just say it."

"Margie told me someone had stopped by PRC to visit with you," Amy spoke softly and Avery couldn't be angry. Amy was the sweetest, kindest soul. "I suppose it came as a shock, seeing him after all this time…" Amy looked to Betsy, who had recently turned eighty and felt it gave her the license to say pretty much anything that came to her mind.

"If by *him* you mean Grayson Stone, yes, he is in town." She sighed and kept her gaze on the cover of her Bible. "And it was a shock."

"He certainly is in town," Franny said. "Does he know?"

"Does he know what?" Avery asked, knowing full well the answer to the question.

"You know…" Franny said.

"There's nothing to do but marry him," Betsy chimed in.

Avery choked on the water she'd been in the process of swallowing. "Marry him?"

"Now, girls," Patsy interceded. "I don't think Avery has asked for our advice."

"People rarely do," Amy said with a cheeky look on

her face. "That doesn't usually stop us from giving advice. The good Lord himself said to not let the sun go down on our anger and we're to forgive."

"We're also not going to use our Bible study to lecture Avery," Nan said. "Avery has always done what is right for her and her daughter, and she'll continue to do so."

Avery gave her foster mom a grateful look. "Thank you."

Patsy made a sound of agreement. "Exactly. We're here to support Avery, Quinn and even Grayson. They're going to need us."

"Marriage," Betsy started.

The door to the kitchen flew open and Quinn ran to their table, laughter sparkling in her dark eyes. Avery's breath caught painfully in her chest at the obvious resemblance between Quinn and Grayson. She'd always seen it, but now, with him home, it became all the more obvious. The ladies at the table seemed to take simultaneous drinks of coffee.

"Mom, there's a donkey running down the street and guess who is chasing it?"

"Grayson," Franny said with a nod. "Hmmm, that is sure a fine-looking man running down the street."

Flora giggled like a schoolgirl and then turned a bright shade of pink. "Oh my, he is handsome. But I don't think he'll catch that donkey on his own."

"We have to help him!" Quinn headed for the front room of the diner.

"He might as well load that thing up and haul it to the auction," Curtis Fisher called out from his table as Avery stood up to follow her daughter.

The other men at the table nodded in agreement, then

started a conversation on how worthless that donkey was and why no self-respecting cattleman would own it.

Avery couldn't agree more but she wasn't going to say it. Instead, she hurried after Quinn, who was already out on the sidewalk and looking for her father and the runaway miniature donkey. He had livestock to care for, he'd told her. If this was his livestock, he deserved to be chasing it around town as punishment for his exaggeration.

"He went thataway," A local farmer said as he came up the sidewalk. "That is, if you're a-looking for Grayson and that donkey. That thing is headed for the river."

The James River, just three blocks from the center of town.

"Thank you, Joe," Avery called back to him. He tipped his hat, revealing his shaggy, thinning gray hair, the same gray as his pointy beard and his brushy mustache.

"Welcome, Avery."

Avery and Quinn hurried down the sidewalk, heading left down River Landing Avenue. The narrow, pothole-filled street led to a small clearing at the edge of the river and a paved boat ramp used for putting boats in and taking them out of the water.

"There he is," Quinn called out as she sped up in the direction of her father and the white donkey with the dark gray spots.

Avery slowed her pace and heaved a deep breath. She wasn't used to running that far. She switched to a fast walk in the direction of Quinn, Grayson and the donkey. Grayson had the animal cornered and Quinn was moving in from the other side. Grayson lifted the lasso he'd been carrying and after a few twirls he let it go, flying through the air in the direction of the donkey.

The donkey couldn't have seen the lasso coming but he must have heard it whistle through the air. His white ears twitched like a TV antenna and then he bolted.

He let out an angry bray and trotted away from his captors, right toward Avery. He stopped in front of her, dropping his head submissively. She didn't want to startle him. As fun as it had been to watch Grayson chasing him, she doubted the run had been much good for the short-legged beast who now gasped for air and seemed completely worn out.

"Do you need water?" she asked.

The donkey raised his head and eyed her speculatively.

"Don't baby that beast." Grayson came toward them, Quinn at his side, grinning as if this might be the most fun she'd ever had. The look on her daughter's face took Avery by surprise.

Grayson removed his cowboy hat and swiped at his forehead. His face was red, and perspiration soaked his dark hair. Sweat darkened his shirt.

Their eyes met and Avery drew in a breath, very aware that her daughter was watching them, and yet, also aware of Grayson in a way that made her doubt her sanity. The moment reminded her too much of her teen self, the girl who had wanted desperately to be loved by him.

She'd grown past that need for his love. She was whole and she'd created a life for herself and for Quinn. She was happy. Content. She had a faith that grounded her.

She swallowed past the emotions that had bubbled

up to the surface, swatting away the feelings that tangled her up in the past.

Grayson shoved the hat back on his head, slipped the loop over the donkey's head and settled it around the animal's neck. Then he winked at her.

She could have gone the rest of her life without that wink.

"You got him," Quinn said proudly, grinning up at Grayson. He was speechless.

But only for a moment.

"I couldn't have done it without you. How did you know I needed help?"

Quinn's face shone with happiness. "I was doing dishes for Tilly and saw you run past."

"I bet that was quite a sight," he said.

She chuckled. "It was pretty funny."

"Well, I'm glad you came to help. Now I have to lead this animal home."

"Could I help?" Quinn asked. She glanced from Grayson to Avery.

That meant allowing her to go back to the farm with Grayson. Avery knew that this had to happen. Eventually. She'd just thought it would be something they'd work up to. One of these days. Not today.

"I…" she started, her gaze connecting with Grayson's. He wore a similar look of hopefulness, matching his daughter's.

"Please," Quinn pleaded. She stopped, managing to paste a contrite look on her face because they had a "no pleading" rule.

"Yes, you may go." Avery barely got the words out and Quinn's arms were around her.

"Thank you, thank you, thank you. You're the best mom." Quinn jumped as she hugged.

"I'll pick you up in a bit."

"Come by for dinner," Grayson suggested. "I can make burgers on the grill. Nan is welcome, too."

Dinner with Grayson. Avery tried to come up with an excuse, a reason why she couldn't make it. But this wasn't about her. This wasn't Grayson asking her out. This was about Quinn building a relationship with her father.

She managed a slight nod. "We can do that."

"Good. I'll see you at five." Grayson handed the rope to their daughter. "Do you want to lead this mangy beast home?"

She nodded rapidly and started walking, the donkey at her side.

"This isn't easy," Avery admitted to Grayson.

He pushed his hat back, giving her a better view of his face. "I know it isn't. I promise I'll keep her safe, Avery, but I need to get to know my daughter. We need an opportunity, the three of us, to figure out how our new family is going to work."

"But we aren't a family, Grayson."

"Maybe not in the conventional sense, but we have to figure out how to be the best parents we can be for our daughter's sake."

He was right, but a teeny tiny part of her wanted to refuse. She wanted to hold on to Quinn. She wanted to protect them both from being hurt. She could see the sincerity in his gaze, but she could also see the doubts. That was the part of Grayson that had changed. Nowadays he doubted himself.

That insecurity eased something inside her and

she nodded, agreeing to his plan. She could do this.
She could give him a chance to know his daughter. She
could spend the evening with him, for Quinn's sake.

Chapter Five

Dragging the donkey home from town hadn't been the easiest job Grayson had ever tackled. It probably ranked at the top of things he would never want to do again. But one thing stood out about the hour it had taken to drag the stubborn beast home: Quinn. She'd made it worth dragging, pushing and bribing the pint-size donkey.

At times she'd held the rope while he pushed from behind. The donkey had often stiffened all four legs and refused to move another inch until they grabbed a handful of grass to lure him another ten, sometimes twenty feet.

They'd tried wrapping the lead rope around the back legs of the animal and pulled to move him forward. They would manage to get him a short distance down the road, then he would either refuse to budge or he would get sidetracked yet again.

Eventually they'd made it home, turned Jack out to pasture with Dolly and Tony, then the two of them had poured tall glasses of sweet tea and sat together on the front porch.

They sat together for a long time, just the two of

them, enjoying the tea and the silence. As the silence went on and on, Grayson didn't know what to say to the girl sitting next to him.

"Who are your friends?" he finally asked her.

She shrugged. "I dunno. Lots of people. I mean, we haven't lived here for very long."

He wondered about that. Were the kids in Pleasant mean to her? Did she get bullied because she didn't have a father or because people suspected he was her dad? He thought about asking but maybe that would be too much too soon.

"I have friends," she said with a serious look. "If that's what you're worried about. I just don't have a best friend yet. But Mom says I will, someday. I don't think she had best friends, though."

She was probably right about that. Avery had always been smart. Smart and quiet and never part of the popular crowd. She'd spent her time alone, studying and ignoring their taunts.

He'd been the bully. And yet, secretly in love with her, as much as someone like him could love anyone.

"Tucker was always her friend," he admitted with no small amount of chagrin. He wasn't proud of the person he'd been. He should have been more like Tucker. Kinder. More decent.

She cocked her head to study him, and looking far too grown up. "Yeah, he and my mom are still friends. He sits with us at church. Tucker and Shay."

"Do they?" Jealousy washed over him, and he cringed. Time to change the subject. "We could start making deviled eggs to go with our burgers. Want to help me?"

"Sure. Do you know how to cook?" She hopped up to follow him into the house.

Grayson held the door open for her.

"I do. It's healthier than eating out and I enjoy it."

"My mom doesn't like to cook. She can but she says it takes a lot of time and planning. We make stuff together. Or we did, until we moved in with Nan. Nan is the best cook ever. She's better than a restaurant."

He grinned. "I bet she is. I always loved her casseroles on Potluck Sundays at church."

"Is Nan bringing a casserole?" His dad shuffled into the kitchen, leaning heavily on his walker until he slid onto a chair.

"No, I'm doing the cooking tonight." Grayson watched as his father got settled. Quinn had taken a seat on a bar stool next to the counter.

"I guess you won't poison us," Mathias grumbled, then he winked at his granddaughter. "What do you think? Should we go ahead and order from Tilly's just in case?"

"I think he can do it," Quinn said, defending his cooking abilities. Then she flashed her dimples at her grandfather. "But I'll keep an eye on him."

"You do that, short stuff. He needs supervising."

"I've been cooking for you for several weeks now," Grayson reminded his father. "You seem to be surviving just fine."

Mathias waggled his shaggy gray eyebrows at his granddaughter. "I suppose he isn't too bad."

Grayson had boiled eggs the previous day. He took them from the fridge and sat the bowl in front of his daughter. "This is your job. Peel the boiled eggs."

She set to work cracking eggs and peeling the shell

off. Grayson rinsed and cut the eggs in half, scooping out the boiled yolks and putting them in a separate bowl.

"What do we do after this?" Quinn asked.

"Smash them, add mayo, a little mustard, salt, sugar and some secret ingredients."

"What's the secret?" She watched as he cut more eggs in half.

He leaned toward her. "You have to promise you won't tell."

She crossed her heart. "I won't."

"French dressing. Just a little."

"California," Mathias grumbled. "That's why he thinks he's a cook. He can't make us just a burger and fries."

"I'll make fries," Grayson promised.

"I can help," Quinn offered. She hopped off the bar stool and moved to his side where she watched him work on the deviled egg mixture. "Can I spoon that into the eggs?"

Mathias chuckled, the sound taking Grayson by surprise. "You look like a skittish colt about to dart off. Where do you get all of that energy?" his dad asked.

She smiled and leaned down to give her grandfather a hug. "You're not so bad."

"You're young yet. You'll learn more as you get older." Mathias gave her back an awkward pat.

"Are you going to help?" Grayson asked his daughter.

With a nod she moved to his side. "What do I do?"

"A spoon of this in each egg."

She took the spoon, scooped up some of the yolk mixture, then lifted it up to her mouth as if she planned to take a bite. He gave her a warning look and she giggled as she filled the hole in the boiled egg half.

The dog began to bark and Grayson could hear the low hum of an engine. He glanced out the kitchen window. It was Avery and Nan. They were early.

"We have company," he said.

"It's Mom and Nan." Quinn scooped up another bit of filling. She handed him the spoon.

Mathias shook his head as she ran out the door. "That one will keep you busy," he said with a twinkle in his eye that took Grayson by surprise.

"Yes, she will. I wish I had more time with her."

"Make the time," his dad warned. "You can't get those ten years back, and for that, I apologize. But you have the rest of your life to be her dad."

"From two thousand miles away."

"I guess that's something you're going to have to figure out," Mathias said, craning his head to see if the women were on their way. Grayson did the same.

Grayson agreed with his father but didn't continue the conversation because it would mean admitting to his own fears. What if he let Avery and Quinn down? What if he couldn't be the person they needed?

His track record at being someone Avery could count on was pretty shaky.

"I'll be back," he told his dad as he walked out the back door.

Quinn was helping Avery and Nan haul a basket out of the backseat. Nan smiled at him as she wrapped an arm around Quinn, who was quickly explaining the process of making deviled eggs.

"Grayson, for the life of me, I couldn't remember your dad being here at the farm. When did he move back?"

Grayson started at the question. Avery looked just as confused.

"We've been here for a few weeks," he responded.

"Well, that's part of getting older." Nan brushed it off, waving her hand as if it was nothing. "I have to make lists and notes all the time, just to keep myself on track."

"Don't feel bad," Grayson told the older woman. "I have to set reminders on my phone. That's how I keep myself on schedule."

"I'll have to look into that." Nan grabbed up her basket. "Come on, Quinn, let's go inside. You can show me those deviled eggs you were making."

Quinn seemed about to argue but Nan gave her a look.

"Okay, fine. And my grandfather is in there, too." Quinn gave them a curious look but she went on to the house with Nan.

"That wasn't too obvious," Avery said as she came round the front of her car with a smaller basket. "Nan insisted on making her green beans. I didn't object. They are the best."

He remembered. They were cooked in bacon grease with a touch of mustard and brown sugar.

"I won't object, either. I've tried for years to replicate that recipe. It's never the same as Nan's." He walked next to Avery. "I'm glad you came."

"I considered standing you up. Payback."

The look on her face wavered between teasing and hurt. He had stood her up? He tried to remember but it was a long time ago and those hadn't been his best days. His memory had holes like Swiss cheese. That didn't usually bother him, but this mattered. He had hurt Avery. He'd left her alone to have their child.

Avery looked up at him, her eyes narrowing to green slits. She wasn't angry, just confused. Then she sighed. "You don't remember?"

"I don't."

"I used to think I was so unimportant that you couldn't be bothered to pick up the phone and call. Now I see that I wasn't even worth remembering."

He needed to tell her, but how? How did he explain his addictions, his past and where life had taken him? He worried that opening up that can of worms would make her doubt his ability to be a father. Make her never be able to trust him or want him in Quinn's life.

"How about if I give you the short version?" she whispered, her gaze shifting to the back door. "Eleven years ago I had just graduated from high school and you'd finished your first year of college."

"I know that," he said. He did remember the time they spent together. Driving back roads, going to the lake, picnics in secluded places.

"Right, of course. You didn't want people to see us together. But I was insistent. If we were going to go out again, you had to have dinner with me at Tilly's. You had to let people see us together in public." Pain ravaged her expression. Eleven years and she still felt hurt by him, by his actions.

"I didn't show."

"You didn't show," she confirmed.

He brushed a hand through his hair, wishing he could take back that night and everything that had happened afterward. He hoped that going forward, he could make it up to her. She was the mother of his daughter. She deserved his very best.

"I'm sorry," he said, and she heard it in his voice. He was sorry. That didn't take away the pain.

"Why didn't you show up?" What had happened that would have made him forget?

"Bad choices," he admitted. "A lot of bad decisions, careless actions, and then my parents bought me a ticket west. They sent me to California."

He hadn't stood her up. Not in the way she'd always imagined. She'd spent years picturing him sneaking out of town, ashamed of their relationship. The teen version of herself had been hurt by his imagined rejection.

"I'm sorry for your bad choices," she managed a smile. "But I spent several years hurt by your rejection."

"It wasn't a rejection," he assured her.

She didn't know how to feel now, with the truth between them. Most of the truth. She felt he was still hiding something but whatever it was, she told herself it didn't matter. Or she hoped it didn't. As long as he didn't hurt Quinn.

"Mom, are you coming in?" Quinn stood on the covered back porch. Hands on her hips, she eyed the two of them.

"Yes, Quinn, we're coming," Avery assured her daughter. Then she looked back at Grayson. "We can talk more later."

"Yes, later."

Before long, Grayson was out in the backyard, cooking burgers on the grill. Nan sat next to the judge, the two talking about the old days of Pleasant and the Stone family home in town. The house had new owners two times over now and it didn't look at all the way it did back when the Stones owned the place.

Avery sat off by herself, watching as Grayson cooked the burgers all the while talking to their daughter. It was a scene that had never played out in their lives. The family, the parents, the laughter. They'd lived a solitary existence, she and Quinn, until coming to Pleasant.

When the hamburgers were ready, they all moved inside. They all sat together in the small dining room of the old farmhouse. The table they ate at was scarred from years of use. The chairs were mismatched. It was not at all the picture of the Stone family that Avery had conjured as a young girl. In her dreams the Stones had eaten in a large dining room in the large brick house in Pleasant. Every meal had been served on china and their tea would have been served in crystal goblets.

She'd often imagined what his parents said to him, and as a child the images had been filled with praise and laughter. As she'd gotten older and learned more about the judge and Mrs. Stone, she'd realized how far off course her imaginings had been. The Stones had acted like they were the perfect family but their home had been anything but happy.

"I heard there are going to be storms in the next few days," Mathias Stone said into the heavy silence that hung over them.

"I'd heard that, too," Nan spoke up. "Of course it'll storm. I've been working on my garden. That never fails to bring a hard rain."

"Like washing a car," Mathias said.

"My art project won an award," Quinn chimed in as she polished off her burger.

"That's amazing. Congratulations." Grayson put an

arm around Quinn's shoulder and gave her a quick hug. The gesture warmed Avery's heart. It was the way a father should treat his daughter. And having a father was important. Avery should know, because she'd never had one, not really. As much as she'd dreaded this moment, when Quinn would turn to Grayson, Avery knew how much it meant. She realized how much she'd kept her daughter from having what she'd always wanted for herself.

"I always loved art. I use it a lot in my business, just not in the same way as I did in art classes," Grayson told their daughter.

"I can't even draw stick figures," Avery admitted. "So now we know where she got her artistic ability."

"Where do you work?" Quinn asked him. "I mean, I'm your daughter and I don't even know what you do or where you live. That's kind of weird."

"I work on buildings." Grayson hadn't thought about the empty spaces in their lives, in their relationship. She loved art and horses and he worked on buildings. They should know these things about each other.

"Buildings?" Quinn prodded.

"When I left Missouri, I had an opportunity to get my life on track. After I figured some things out, I went to work for my uncle in California. He was a Realtor but also a contractor, building homes and designing housing developments. I went to school and became an architect."

Mathias made a face. "Don't let him fool you. He's a big builder out there in California. Bought himself a ranch outside Monterey."

"A small acreage," Grayson corrected.

He'd gotten his life on track? What had happened

to Grayson when he left Pleasant? Yes, he'd alluded to trouble but it seemed he'd left out some details. Avery glanced out the window, her thoughts wandering down lonely paths that made her question herself, question Grayson and even question what they were doing here together.

Suddenly, out the window she noticed something moving. "There's a llama in your yard," she said.

"Uh-oh, it's Tony Llama!" Quinn scooted her chair back and hurried out the door.

"Wait for us," Grayson warned.

"You can't say those animals haven't livened the place up," Mathias cackled. "You can't get rid of them now. My granddaughter likes them too much."

Nan started clearing the table. "You all go chase animals. Mathias and I will watch from the back porch. We'll try to save you a piece of pie."

"I can help clean up," Avery offered. It didn't come easy, backing off and giving Grayson this time with their daughter. "I'm sure you and Quinn can get them all in just as easily without me."

"I don't know," Mathias spoke in his halting speech. "The llama doesn't like men."

"That's okay. I'm not too fond of him, either." Grayson headed for the back door. "I think we can get them. If we're not back soon, come check on us."

After she'd gathered up the plates, she found herself smiling as he stood with his hand on the door handle, about to go out. He'd shoved a white cowboy hat on his head and he was watching her, his cheeks dimpling. The plates wobbled and she tightened her hold on the stoneware and on her emotions.

This would never do. Having feelings for Grayson had never gotten her anything but heartache.

"Go," she told him.

"Right," he said. "We'll be back for pie."

Fifteen minutes later Quinn returned without Grayson. Nan had washed the dishes and Avery had dried and put them away as Mathias entertained them with stories from his life in the retirement community in Springfield.

"Where's your dad?" Mathias asked as he handed Quinn a package of cookies. "You look like you might need these."

"We chased them," she said, out of breath. "But we finally got them in."

"That's good," Nan said.

"They're all in but the llama has a cut on his side, from going through the fence. My dad is doctoring him. Or trying."

Avery got stuck on the word *dad*. It literally took her breath. Nan elbowed her, reminding her to breathe.

"I'll go help him," Avery said. She didn't know a thing about doctoring animals, but she did know that she needed a moment to come to grips with the reality that Quinn would, of course, call Grayson "Dad."

"I'll go, too." Quinn took a cookie from the package and started to follow.

"Not so fast, kiddo." Nan tossed her a towel. "You can help me finish up."

Avery walked out the back door and followed the worn path out to the barn. The basset hound trotted along next to her. She smiled as it suddenly hit her that this was Grayson's life for the time being. His family farm with his father, a group of runaway animals and a slinky of a dog.

"What are you smiling at?" Grayson asked as he came out of the barn, his hat tipped low, blocking the late-afternoon sun.

"The dog, the llama and the miniature duo."

"Ah, I can see how that would be funny." He took her hand and led her into the barn. "Tony doesn't like to be doctored."

"It probably stings him," she offered. "Does he need stitches?"

"No, he's fine. I sprayed it with some antibacterial medicine and turned him loose. I'll doctor him again tomorrow, to make sure it doesn't get infected. I guess Doc Lincoln is still around if it needs more than the spray."

"I came out to help, but I guess you don't need any," she said, suddenly embarrassed by her quick escape to the barn. To him.

"Thank you." He pushed the hat back and surveyed her with a steady look in his autumn-brown eyes. "We haven't talked specifics, but I guess this is as good a time as any to discuss the fact that I want to be a part of Quinn's life."

"I know you do."

He stood there silent for a moment. Then asked, "What if I mess up?"

She found the question puzzling. "I'm not sure how you would mess up. I mean, as parents, one thing I can guarantee you is, you will always mess up. I've obviously messed up."

His gaze turned tender but she deserved anger. She'd kept him from his daughter. That decision weighed heavily on her heart. Her fears had kept Grayson from his daughter.

"But you're not a…a…" he stammered as he reached for her hand, lacing his fingers through hers. "I've said these words so many times and yet, today, saying them to you is the most difficult thing I think I've ever had to do. I'm an addict, Avery. I'm clean, but I'm no one's hero."

The words took her by surprise. "I'm sorry? What?"

"I'm an addict. I didn't leave town by choice years ago. I left because my parents sent me to California where I spent several months in rehab getting my life together. I've been clean for nine years, Avery. But now I have more than just myself to worry about, so I have to be honest about who I am."

He looked so heartbroken and worried that she had to reach out and comfort him. He'd opened up to her. As hurt as she'd been, as much as she still didn't trust him, she found herself wanting him to be his very best, for Quinn's sake.

"I wish I had known," she said. "I guess I should have known."

"Hardly anyone knew. I was pretty good at hiding it. But I'm telling you all of this because I need for you to forgive me."

"I forgave you a long time ago, Grayson. We both made mistakes, not just you."

She could forgive him. She could admit that Quinn needed him. She didn't want to be hurt by him. His admission, however honest, had just released a whole new set of doubts.

Doubts that were overcome by other feelings. In the space of a heartbeat, memories returned to taunt her.

He'd always been captivating to her. He'd always been more than she could ever have. A dream, always out of reach.

He leaned in, drawing close, stealing her breath. His lips brushed hers and she closed her eyes, losing herself in a moment that she should have avoided.

But she didn't want to. She wanted his arms holding her close.

Because all of the years, all of the hurt, all of it evaporated when he held her in his arms. Hadn't it always been that way?

The kiss ended and she pulled away. She should know better than to get caught up in the way he made her feel. She'd learned her lessons and moved on.

Or so she thought.

"I should go," she stammered.

"No." He reached for her hand. "Avery, don't go. I'm sorry for…"

"Don't be. I kissed you back, Grayson. But we can't do this. Let's focus on Quinn and remember that she's the reason we are back in each other's lives. Neither of us wants to revisit the past because that's just a place of pain."

He stared at her for a moment, then nodded.

"I agree."

"I have to go," she said again.

She had to go because the kiss had reminded her how easily she'd always been able to overlook the hurt he'd caused her. She'd always wanted him so much that she'd been willing to overlook the red flags: the things he'd said, the way he'd treated her.

For years she'd convinced herself that she'd grown

up, gotten past being that naive young girl. Their kiss had proved otherwise.

On the bright side, at least she'd recognized it and knew when it was time to walk away.

Chapter Six

"Is Grayson coming in today?" Laura called out as Avery passed by her office at PRC on Wednesday morning.

"Not today. His father had an appointment in Springfield."

Since the previous Saturday, Avery had distanced herself from Grayson. It hadn't been easy, not when Quinn wanted to see him daily. They needed to find a balance, but it was easier said than done. He was new and fun, the parent who didn't have to tell their daughter no. That had to change. And soon.

"Why the serious face?" Laura left her office and walked alongside Avery down the hallway.

"Are you following me?"

Laura gave her a sheepish grin. "Not really. I mean, I do want the story but I'm also taking some paperwork to Mrs. Culver."

"There is no story." Avery paused at the door to Margie's room. The older woman smiled up from her knitting. "How are you feeling?"

"Curious," Margie said. "I feel very curious. You

haven't stopped in to talk to me this week. I'm more than blood pressure and medication, you know."

Avery stepped into the room and sat in the chair next to Margie's bed. "You're right. You're far more than vitals and meds. You're cookies and apples and someone who always took time to talk to me. Thank you for reminding me."

"Oh." Margie put a cool hand over Avery's hand. "Stop being so serious. You know that I'm not going anywhere. I'll be here anytime you need to talk."

"Thank you. And there really isn't much to tell. Grayson Stone is home in Pleasant, but only temporarily. He met Quinn last week and they've really hit it off."

"He's always been charming," Margie said to Laura, not Avery.

"Charming isn't everything," Avery grumbled.

Margie patted her hand. "No, but knowing his daughter is. I'm not wrong, am I?"

Avery briefly closed her eyes. There were no secrets in a small town. "You're not wrong."

"What is that noise?" Laura stepped out into the hall. "It's raining. A lot."

Wind slammed against the window, causing them all to jump.

"We need to check the weather." Avery left her seat next to Margie. "I really dislike storms."

"It's May in Missouri," Margie reminded. "It'll pass soon enough."

Avery pulled Margie's blanket up and patted the frail hand that held her knitting needles. "I'll be back."

Avery and Laura hurried down the hall as they heard thunder crashing outside the building, rattling the windows.

"What's going on out there?" Avery asked.

Residents and staff were gathered around a television in the lobby. The red outlines of nearby counties were a warning of tornadoes in the area. Not mere watches with favorable conditions, but warnings to take cover. The storms that roared outside might be a precursor for worse storms to come.

"What should we do?" Avery asked the administrator as he came out of his office to join them. Mr. Davis, middle-aged and a steady force in their establishment, nodded as he watched the broadcast.

"Let's start moving people to the central hallway. All hands on deck. Whatever wing you're assigned to, you're responsible for getting those residents there. Bring pillows and blankets. Those who can't be moved, close the blinds, pull curtains and move the beds as far from the window as possible."

It was the best they could do, and they all knew that it wouldn't be completely effective. Still, with smiles on their faces and no time to waste, they began to move residents. As the rain pounded and the wind started howling louder as it picked up speed, they kept a steady stream of residents, some mobile and some in need of more help, moving to the hallway.

Margie brought her knitting with her. As she continued working on the blanket, she started to sing about God's protection. Other voices, some weak and some strong, joined hers.

As Avery helped move residents as quickly yet safely as she could, she tried very hard not to think about Quinn and Nan. She prayed as she worked, begging God to keep them safe, pleading with Him to protect them all.

Her fear must have shown on her face because when she finally took shelter in the area where Margie had been moved, she reached for her hand.

"Fear not, Avery." Margie smiled up at her. "He's got this storm and all of the other storms in His very capable hands."

"I know." Avery leaned down to hug the woman who had been a Sunday school teacher and a compassionate figure in her life for as long as Avery could remember.

The tornado sirens drifted through the noise of the storm. The haunting sound whirred through the air.

"This isn't fun," sweet Camilla Bolling whispered. "I'm not sure who thought this would be fun, but it isn't. Is this a party?"

"Hush, it's a tornado," Carlin, an older gentleman, shouted. "We're going to be blown to Kansas and back."

"Shhh." Laura put a hand on Carlin's shoulders. "We're all listening to Margie's song."

"Margie can't sing," Carlin growled. "What's her God going to do for us now?"

"Keep us safe!" Anita Brooks pointed a finger at Carlin. "Why do you always have to be such a grouch? Scaring children, throwing rocks at dogs and now being mean to the elderly."

"Oh, be quiet, Anita." Carlin grabbed the blanket off his lap and pulled it over his head. But beneath the blanket Avery thought she heard him say a prayer.

They all prayed as the wind buffeted the building. A crashing sound echoed through the halls, deafening in its intensity. People screamed but the sounds were lost in the roar of the storm.

As Avery moved among the residents, helping them to cover themselves with their pillows and blankets, she prayed for her daughter. She prayed for God to watch over their community, the residential home, her family and the school.

Those who could were curled against the wall. Laura reached for her hand. "Avery, you have to take shelter."

"I have to make sure everyone is safe."

The building seemed to shake and tiles fell from the ceiling. Avery hurried to make sure no heads were uncovered. More tiles fell.

"God, protect us from the storm," Margie and Anita cried out in unison. A gruff voice said, "Amen." Carlin.

It seemed like hours but it might have only been minutes until the storm passed over. The winds calmed. Quiet blanketed Hall C except for soft cries and murmured prayers.

"I think it's over," Avery said. She looked to John, one of their aides. "Let's make a check of the facility and call 911. I have a feeling we're probably going to need help."

"Avery, you need to get cleaned up." John touched her forehead. "That's a pretty good gash."

"I'm fine. I'll take care of it later."

"I don't think later is going to work." John glanced around at the residents, most of whom were coming out from under their blankets and pillows. He motioned to Laura. "Can you get her cleaned up, please? She won't do us much good if she's unconscious."

"I'm not going to be unconscious," she argued.

"Of course not."

A door opened at the end of the hall, giving them a view of outside. Downed trees were everywhere, and parts of buildings that didn't belong to them were scattered nearby. Avery swayed and suddenly Laura was at her side.

"We need to make sure everyone is okay."

"You need to stop for a minute and take care of yourself," Laura told her.

"I'm fine."

"You're not fine."

Avery put a gloved hand to her forehead and it came away sticky with her own blood. "It's just a cut."

"It's more than a cut, but you're not going to listen to me."

"No, I'm not." Avery had over one hundred people counting on her to keep them safe. Their families counted on her. And all the while, she was thinking of Quinn and praying she was safe.

Mr. Davis appeared in the doorway at the end of the hall. "Everyone okay in here?"

Laura pointed to Avery.

"We're good. Some cuts and bruises. How is the building?" Avery asked as she maneuvered around residents to reach her boss.

"The building seems to be fine other than a few broken windows and the ceiling tiles that shook loose in here. We tried 911 but cell phones aren't working and landlines are also down. Are you okay?" he asked.

"Fine." Avery took a piece of gauze John handed her and she held it to her forehead. "Where do you want us to start?"

Mr. Davis gave her a cautious look, and she knew he was concerned.

"I'm fine. I promise you. I need to get this done so I can go check on my daughter."

"I understand. I'm going to start by having aides

and our maintenance man check each room to make sure they're habitable. We can move residents to rooms that are safe and make notes on rooms that aren't. All residents without a room can be taken to the activity rooms."

Avery agreed, then started mobilizing aides to begin assessing the residents to make sure there were no injuries or secondary issues related to the storm. Fear and anxiety were a real concern.

She glanced toward the end of the hall and unexpected relief flooded her at the sight of Grayson. She ran over to him.

"Have you been to the elementary school?"

"No, I haven't. I just got back into town with my dad. He's in the car with Nina. The road into town is blocked."

With no phone service and no way to reach her daughter or Nan, fear started rising up and eating away at the calm she'd managed to maintain since the storm hit.

"I need to get to my daughter," Avery said, glancing around the crowded halls where residents waited to be returned to rooms.

"Let me bring Dad and Nina inside, and I'll help you get things settled in here."

"Thank you, Grayson." She stepped back as he leaned in and took a closer look at her forehead.

"Looks like a nasty cut. I think you might need to let someone take care of that."

"I can take care of myself."

"Right, of course. I'll grab Dad and Nina. And I'll see what I can do about sending someone to check on Nan and Quinn."

Avery watched him walk out the front door of the center before heading to the medical supply closet. She found what she needed, not only for herself but for the residents who might be injured. In one of the bathrooms nearby, she washed her hands with antiseptic soap at the sink, pulled on clean gloves and tended to the gash on her head. It wasn't long, maybe an inch, but it was deep.

The door to the room opened. Grayson had returned. He watched her for a moment, then he took the butterfly bandage from her. "Let me."

"No, it's fine, I can…ouch!"

"I'm sorry, sweetheart."

"Don't call me *sweetheart*." She closed her eyes and whispered, "I'm worried about them."

"I know you are. So am I. I'm sure they're fine. But as soon as I can, I'll get to them."

"I need to be with her. Both of them."

"I know." He pressed a kiss to her temple. "We can't get to her right now, but we can pray."

She nodded. And then he prayed, taking her by surprise.

When had he become so strong in his faith? When had he become the man she could trust herself to lean on? Another mystery of Grayson Stone yet to be answered.

Grayson left the room, with Avery walking out before him. She seemed composed but he knew what that tightness around her mouth, the shadows in her green eyes, meant. He felt the same fear.

The hardest part was not being able to do more. As a dad, even one as late to the game as he was, he felt a need to move heaven and earth to get to his child.

"How can I help out here?" he asked.

"We need to start checking rooms for any damage, then getting residents back to their beds. It's lunchtime and some of our people need to take their medication."

"I'll start looking over the rooms. You take care of medications. I'll take someone with me. They can move people as soon as I check a room."

"Thank you, again."

"Staying busy will help us both," he assured her. "Nina is an LPN, as well. If you need her for anything, she said to let her know."

Avery assigned Laura to help him evaluate rooms. She could quickly let them know who could be returned to their rooms and who would need an alternative. Grayson led her from room to room, checking windows, ceilings and walls for any signs of damage. She took notes and then called out names and room numbers to staff that were waiting for orders.

He had finished one hallway when he noticed fire trucks and other emergency vehicles outside. He headed for the side door and pushed it open. He'd never been so glad to see first responders, but more than that—Tucker Church climbing out of a fire truck.

Of course Tucker would be a volunteer.

"Is everyone okay in there?" Tucker asked as he approached, pulling on a bright yellow vest and a hard hat.

"I think so. What about town? We can't reach Nan at the house or Quinn at school."

Tucker took him by the arm and pulled him away from Laura and other staff that had come outside. "The school is damaged. There's scattered damage all over town. Trees, power lines, maybe a dozen homes damaged."

"Any injuries?" Grayson asked, afraid to know the answer.

"At the school, yes. They're triaging the wounded and connecting parents to students."

As they talked, several cars were pulling up. The people getting out seemed to be nurses and other staff.

"We contacted staff that we knew personally and they've also brought in help from surrounding areas," Tucker explained. "You and Avery should go. The road to town has been cleared. You can get through now."

"Thank you. I owe you, man." Grayson shook Tucker's hand.

"I wish I could do more."

Grayson hurried back inside. He found Avery hovering over a patient. He waited patiently while she checked vitals, and asked a few questions.

"What is it?" she asked, finally looking at him.

"Tucker is here. He said the road to town is clear and we should go."

"Go where? Grayson, what's wrong?"

"The elementary school was damaged. If you give me your keys, I'll have Nina drive my dad home. We can take my truck and head to Pleasant."

Suddenly, her body started to tremble. "I've been fine all this time, but now I'm really worried for my daughter."

"I know. Me, too."

They found Mr. Davis. He was assigning jobs to those who had arrived to help. He saw them and nodded.

"Go, go. You don't have to ask. Go check on Quinn. We have more staff coming in."

"What about your family, Mr. Davis?" Avery asked.

"My wife and son just showed up. They're safe and our home is fine."

Within minutes, Grayson had his dad and Nina out the door, and he and Avery were in his truck on the road to town. The damage was immediately noticeable. Trees were scattered everywhere; power lines were down and there were parts of roofs and sheet metal wrapped in trees.

As they drove, he could hear Avery's whispered prayers filling his truck's cab.

As they neared the school, the damage became more extensive. Lights flashed as emergency crews worked. People, shell-shocked by what had transpired, stood in their yards, looking at what had befallen their community.

"This is terrible," Avery whispered. "How did this happen? It was just raining."

"I know." Grayson reached out and grabbed her hand in his. "She's okay."

"I know." She sobbed a little, covering her face with her right hand. "I hope. I keep telling myself she's okay but then I think, what if…?"

"She's fine." It came out a little more harshly than he'd intended.

The driveway to the school was blocked by police and first responders. They directed people to park down the street. Grayson pulled into the first space he came to. His truck had barely stopped and Avery had jumped out. He followed, catching up with her.

"We have to be calm," he warned as he took hold of her hand to slow her pace. "Avery, for Quinn, we have to be calm."

Her steps faltered. "I know. I really do. But I keep

thinking of my daughter inside that school, frightened, possibly injured. And Nan. I can't reach Nan."

"Tucker is sending someone to check on Nan. As far as he knows, there's no damage in that area."

They reached the front of the school and saw that they weren't the only parents who had gathered. School administrators were organizing the crowds, explaining the process for connecting students with their parents.

Parents with injured children would be taken to a triage area. Ambulances were transporting seriously wounded kids to nearby hospitals. The superintendent continued to announce the protocol and Grayson could see the lines of uninjured children coming from the building.

Grayson continued to hold tight to Avery as they waited for their daughter. This was family, he realized. It came with a lot of responsibility. A family came with people who relied on him to always be his best.

His thoughts started to race down a dangerous path. Today he was someone they could rely on. What if next week he wasn't? For a recovering addict, what-ifs could lead you down the rabbit hole.

As they stood there looking frantically at the groups of children emerging from the building, not seeing Quinn, he knew he wasn't the only one with a future at stake. He wasn't the only one depending on him to be sober, to be clean, to make the right choices each and every day.

Grayson's perfect plan for coming home long enough to get his father settled had become anything but perfect and far from simple. He'd come back to Pleasant as the happily single son, eager to take care of his father. His new role of father had changed everything. As a man who always liked to have a plan, he had no plan for this situation. He didn't have a plan for being Quinn's dad and he definitely didn't have a plan for handling Avery in his life.

While these thoughts were swirling through his head, he realized that they were being directed to go to the triage area, where the injured students were waiting to be taken to area hospitals. Avery clung to him, cutting off the circulation in his hand, expecting him to be the strong one.

Please, Lord, help me to be someone she can count on.

Chapter Seven

The moment she saw her daughter, Avery pulled away from Grayson and ran to Quinn's side. Her baby girl was lying on a stretcher, her face pale, her eyes closed. She touched Quinn's hand, her bruised face. While she'd been doing her job, her daughter had been here injured and alone.

"Quinn, honey, Mommy is here."

"Mommy," Quinn whispered, licking her lips. "It was scary."

"I know. I was scared, too." Avery kissed her daughter's cheek gently. Grayson stood behind her. Glancing up at him, she noticed he was rocking back and forth and looked unsure. "Your dad is here."

Quinn blinked at him, then half smiled. She grimaced in pain. Avery glanced around, looking for a medic, someone to tell her the reasons why her daughter was on this stretcher. Grayson's hand on her shoulder reminded her to stay calm.

Just then, a paramedic approached them. "Are you Quinn's parents?"

"We are," they said in unison.

The paramedic pulled on clean gloves as she spoke. "We're going to transport her to Springfield. She was unconscious for several minutes. No broken bones. She was just a little confused when she woke up. Do you have a preference for which hospital?"

Avery gave them the name of the hospital, then slid her hand into Grayson's. The gesture was automatic and necessary. It seemed the only way to hold on and to keep from falling apart.

"We'll be loading her and leaving in a few minutes," the paramedic assured them. "We'll take good care of her."

"Of course. We'll follow you up there," Grayson assured the paramedic.

Avery leaned close to Quinn. "I'll meet you at the hospital. You're safe and you'll be fine."

"Can't I just go home?" Quinn's bottom lip trembled and a tear trickled down her cheek.

"I'm afraid not, sweetheart. But I'll be right behind you. I'll be with you as soon as possible."

Quinn nodded as her eyes closed. "I'm scared, Mommy."

"I know, sweetie. But I promise you everything will be okay."

Grayson squatted next to their daughter. "Let's pray before you go."

Quinn nodded and Grayson reached for her hand. At that moment his role as father, as protector, as someone they could count on, was the most important thing in the world.

The paramedics gave them their moment, and when they were done, they loaded Quinn on the waiting ambulance. Avery stood next to Grayson and watched as their daughter was driven away in the vehicle, lights flashing.

"Let's go," Grayson told her. "She's going to need us there with her."

Tucker called him while they were driving. That meant at least some phone lines were up and working again. He told them that Nan was fine. But the farm didn't have electricity. He'd convinced her to let him take her to the judge's place, because Mathias Stone's old farmhouse was safe and still had power.

Avery closed her eyes and leaned back against the headrest.

"It could have been worse."

"That's really optimistic." She gazed out the side window, resting her forehead against the cool glass. "Has anyone checked on my house?"

"Not that I know of. I'll be honest. It was the last thing on my mind."

"Mine, too." She reached to turn down the radio. "I can't take much more of the news."

"I agree," Grayson said.

They drove in silence until they finally reached Springfield. Grayson turned on the road that led to the hospital, and soon they were in the parking lot, following arrows to the emergency room.

"I'm glad you're here, Grayson," she told him as they walked through the parking garage. "It would have been very lonely and frightening to do this by myself."

"I'm glad I'm here, too."

All sorts of dark thoughts threatened to rob her of the thin strand of peace she'd been clinging to. She pushed those thoughts aside. She wasn't alone. Grayson was here. Quinn would be fine. She kept repeating that to herself until she believed it.

They entered the emergency room and approached the front desk. "We're Quinn Hammons's parents," Grayson said to the receptionist.

"Okay." The young woman typed into the computer. "Have a seat."

"We'd like to see our daughter," Grayson said, his voice taking on an edge of anger.

"As soon as I can, I'll get you back there. While you're waiting, if you could fill out this information for me…"

Grayson opened his mouth to speak again. Avery had to put a hand on his arm to stop him. She took the electronic tablet from the woman and shot him a warning look.

"Give it a few minutes," she told him.

"She's only ten years old and she's alone," he said.

If she hadn't been so worried, too, she might have smiled at his outrage. "Yes, but she's with doctors and nurses right now. She isn't alone."

She entered Quinn's information into the tablet, handed it back to the woman and led Grayson to a couple of chairs in the waiting area. Aqua-blue chairs in an aqua-blue room. Magazines on the table were about hunting, fishing and local restaurants.

"Mr. and Mrs. Hammons?" A nurse appeared by the sliding doors that led to the exam rooms. "If you want to come with me…"

Grayson tossed a magazine on the table and stood, not waiting for Avery. She caught up with him in a few strides. The nurse led them down a blue hallway to a gray hallway. Quinn was in a room with glass doors, the tan curtains pulled closed. A doctor was examining her as they entered.

"Mr. and Mrs. Hammons, I'm Dr. Sylvester. Quinn and I have been talking about her experience today. It sounds as if they had a day of school they'll never forget." He smiled down at Quinn. "We're going to do a CT scan, and I'm inclined to go ahead and put her in a room tonight, for observation. She's had a pretty rough day and it'll be good to keep an eye on her. I'm assuming you do have a safe place to go with her tomorrow?"

"I…yes, our home…" She looked at Grayson, who had accepted his role as "Mr. Hammons."

"Our home wasn't damaged in the storm," he assured the doctor.

"I'm glad to hear that. The two of you can wait here. If we have a room ready before the CT is finished, I'll have someone let you know and give you the room number."

"Thank you, Doctor," Avery managed to say. She moved to her daughter's side. "You're okay."

"I know," Quinn said. "I'm just sleepy. And hungry."

"That's always a good sign," said Dr. Sylvester. "Once we have you settled, we'll get you something to eat. It probably won't be a cheeseburger."

"I do like cheeseburgers but I feel kind of sick." Suddenly, she leaned over the side of the bed, barely missing the doctor's very expensive shoes.

Avery grabbed a trash can and supported her daughter's head.

"Can they give her something for the nausea?" she asked.

"Yes, let me take care of that." Dr. Sylvester glanced

at his shoes, grinning. "That was pretty impressive aim."

Quinn mumbled an apology. He told her not to worry and then he told her a story that made her smile. An attendant came in to take her to get the CT scan, and pushed her gurney from the room.

Grayson and Avery returned to the waiting area but they didn't get to sit down. The receptionist pointed them in the direction of an alcove with several chairs. Tucker, Nan, Judge Stone and Nina were all waiting.

"We couldn't let you all sit up here alone," Tucker said. "We wanted to check on Quinn. How is she?"

Avery nodded, but her throat tightened and she couldn't make any words come out of her mouth.

"She's fine," Grayson jumped in. "They're doing a CT scan on her, and then they're going to keep her overnight."

"I don't know why we couldn't just take her home. I know she'd prefer her own bed." Nan seemed adamant. Avery was confused by it.

"Nan, we don't have electricity at the house."

Nan blinked. "I know that, but we do have flash-lights and candles."

"You can all stay with us until your power is back on," Judge Stone offered. "We have plenty of room in that old farmhouse. It isn't fancy but it'll keep a roof over our heads."

"Thank you, Judge Stone. That's very generous of you." Avery gave him a gentle smile and started to turn the offer down. But she quickly realized she couldn't, though. They would need a place to stay. And where else could they go?

"Mr. and Mrs. Hammons?" An aide approached cautiously. "We have a room for your daughter. If you want, I can lead you all up there."

"That's mighty nice," the judge said.

Avery gave him a curious look. Once upon a time, she had been driven off his porch when she'd tried to tell him she was pregnant. Now here he was, opening up his home to her and her daughter. He wanted to be here with Quinn. She shouldn't harbor any resentment for their past. She should be thrilled, for Quinn's sake.

"Who is Mr. Hammons?" Tucker whispered to Grayson.

"We are Quinn's parents," Avery addressed the aide. "And we appreciate the offer but I'm familiar with the hospital. Could you just give us the wing and room number?"

The man gave them careful directions to Quinn's room. Glancing at the group of visitors, he also gave them the directions to the waiting area nearest to Quinn.

Avery instantly felt the tension easing. Quinn would be okay. Grayson was with them. They had family here. Or friends who were like a family. Right now she wasn't worried about what would happen next week or next month. It was better to take things one day at a time.

God's word told her not to worry about tomorrow. Worry wouldn't change a thing about her circumstances or her life. She'd always relied on those verses in Matthew and now wasn't the time to forget. Worry wouldn't change their circumstances but faith could.

Grayson's hand grasped hers. She wasn't alone. And it felt right.

Grayson's heart caught in his throat as he sat in the darkened room watching his daughter and her mother as they caught a few fitful hours of sleep. He hadn't been able to close his eyes once. He had needed to watch Quinn, to make sure that she was all right.

"Hey," Avery said as the gray dawn light spread across the eastern sky. Her blond hair framed her face and her green eyes held a sleepy haze.

"Hey," he answered.

She rubbed her hands down her sleepy face, then she quickly redid her messy bun. With narrowed eyes she studied him. "Did you sleep at all?"

"No. I couldn't." He let his gaze track back to their daughter. She still slept, although she had tossed and turned through the night, sometimes making a sound that indicated she was in pain.

Her concussion had been mild. He didn't want to argue with doctors but as far as he was concerned, no injury to his daughter would ever be mild.

Every few hours a nurse had come in to check her vitals. He'd asked once or twice if Quinn might need something for pain. The nurse had been very sympathetic, still calling him Mr. Hammons as they assured him she might have a headache but she would be fine in a few days' time.

"You need sleep, Grayson." Avery moved her lounger chair to an upright sitting position. She smiled at their sleeping daughter.

"She's a pretty perfect kid," he told Avery. "You did an amazing job with her, raising her to be so solid, confident, happy."

"I had a lot of help. From Nan," she said.

"Right, of course. But most of it has been you. Thing is, I'm not sure where I fit in."

Quinn started stirring but didn't wake up.

"I need coffee. Let's walk down the hall and see what we can find." Avery stood and he followed her to the door.

But he couldn't let the conversation drop. "Seriously, Avery, where do I fit in here? I couldn't stop thinking about it all night."

"When you should have been sleeping," she teased him.

Yeah, he should have gotten some sleep. But how could he sleep when his daughter looked so pale, so fragile, in her hospital bed? Not to mention Avery, curled up in a chair, her hand on her daughter's as she dozed.

"No way could I sleep," he told her.

They approached the nurses' station on the floor. She smiled at all the nurses and techs and she asked about coffee. They pointed her to a break room down the hall with coffee, snack cakes, crackers and chips.

A few minutes later Avery poured herself a cup of coffee.

"Grayson, you're her father. I couldn't be both mom and dad, even though I tried. She needed you. I just didn't realize that you were the thing missing from her life. You fit."

Not in Avery's life, he noticed, just in Quinn's. At least it was something. It was a start, a place to begin.

"Do you want some coffee?" she asked, holding up the pot.

He grabbed a paper cup and she poured it for him. "Thank you. For the coffee and for letting me be a part of her life. It was unexpected, but I'm glad to be here."

He fit in his daughter's life. The truth of that washed over him, warm and unexpectedly fulfilling. As if

Quinn was the thing he'd been waiting for to make his life complete.

As long as he didn't mess up, he would be the father she needed. But what if he did mess up? What if nine years of clean living was all for nothing and he slipped?

"What are you thinking about?" Avery asked him as they walked down the silent hallway.

"Nothing," he assured her. Then he decided to be honest. "I'm worried about the future, about being the kind of father she needs me to be."

"If you can't do it, then say so now. Because I don't want you to make her think you're in her life for good, and then something happens and you disappear."

The way he'd disappeared from her life eleven years ago. They stood in the hall for a difficult few minutes.

"I'm in her life." No question. Quinn's life was where he belonged.

They reentered Quinn's room and his gaze landed on the sleeping form of his daughter. Now that he was in her life, she would expect things from him. If he messed up, he'd hurt her. He'd hurt Avery.

Avery was right to question him, to hold him accountable. There was always a chance he would fail, that he would let them both down.

But being a father meant so much to him; he knew he would fight for them. He would fight to stay clean and sober, and to be here for his daughter. And for Avery.

One day at a time.

Chapter Eight

They kept Quinn through the end of the day. Dr. Sylvester had insisted on watching her closely to make sure she was ready to be released. He thought that considering the situation in Pleasant, even a mild concussion needed to be treated cautiously. Avery appreciated his concern. But Quinn was impatient. She wanted to go home, to make sure all of the animals were safe and that her friends were okay. When they were finally released, Avery pushed Quinn in the wheelchair they insisted she use until she got outside. The nurse walked with them to make sure everything went well. Grayson had gone to get the truck.

Grayson had been awfully quiet throughout the day. She had allowed him his peace because he'd seemed to need it. The idea that he had a daughter, that sometimes bad things could happen to her, had all hit him this morning. She knew well what that felt like. She'd been hit by the same realities over the years as Quinn grew up. Each time they experienced a new obstacle or faced another milestone, parenting took on a new dimension. She wanted to reassure him this was all perfectly normal, but a part of her held back, holding on to the boundaries she needed in order to protect herself.

"I'd like to check my home site, to make sure it survived the storm," she told Grayson as they got closer to Pleasant.

Not that it was really a house, not yet. It was a frame, a beginning. They drove in silence for several minutes. She thought he hadn't heard but then he nodded. "Yes, we'll stop by and check it out."

Ten minutes later they pulled down the rutted dirt drive that led to her building site. It was easy to see what was missing. The house, what there had been of it, was gone. The frame had been tossed about like kindling, boards scattered in all directions. Avery couldn't breathe.

"Where's our house?" A groggy Quinn spoke up from the backseat.

"Shhh, go back to sleep." Avery opened the door as the truck rolled to a stop. She wasn't surprised when the back door of the truck cab swung open. "Quinn, stay where you are."

"But I want to go."

"You just got out of the hospital, so please do not leave the truck." Grayson said, appearing at Avery's side. "There are going to be nails and debris that you have to watch for."

Avery surveyed the remains of what would have been their home. It was now just a foundation, nothing more. She had to step over the boards, beams and other materials that had once made up the frame.

She choked at the sight of the nearby dogwood tree that she'd loved so much. When they began to build the house and needed to level the area, she had made sure they didn't touch that tree. Now it was split and broken and most of the limbs were missing. Grayson touched her back, guiding her away from all the debris, the nails, the roofing, scattered about.

"It was going to be our home."

"It will be your home, Avery. You'll start over."

She shook her head. "No."

He slid an arm around her waist and pulled her close. She didn't pull away. In fact, she rested her head on his shoulder. Growing up, he'd never been a true friend to her; maybe he still wasn't. How could she trust him now?

She reminded herself that he'd been with her for two of the worst days of her life. He hadn't left her side all night. He hadn't called someone else to drive her home. He'd been with her at their daughter's side. That meant something.

"Why wouldn't you rebuild, Avery? You're not a quitter." His words broke through the barriers she'd built up since yesterday, seeing her baby injured after the storm.

Tears streamed down her cheeks. She brushed them away, wishing to erase evidence of her weakness. She might be brave, but she wasn't wise.

She'd lost her nest egg.

"My contractor left the state. He took my money and ran off. I was contacted a few days ago by a county deputy. My contractor bilked several people out of money. His bank account is empty. His home is empty. He abandoned his office. He's gone. I have a loan but it won't be enough to rebuild the house I had planned. I've lost the initial money," she admitted, shaking her head. "He did have good recommendations. I checked him out first."

"You're not the first person to get conned like this."

She shuddered. "I really dislike that word. Conned. I'm a smart person. I'm educated. How could this have happened?"

"It happens." He turned her away from the building. "The good news is, I know a guy and so do you. A guy who is more than willing to help you rebuild."

"You were right all along. The house wasn't sturdy and my contractor took advantage of my lack of knowledge. But I'm not going to ask you to build my house, Grayson. I know you have your life and your business to return to back in California."

"But I want to help you."

He wanted to help. But this mess, it was hers. He hadn't gotten her into this. He wasn't responsible for the storm or her mistakes.

"We should probably go. Quinn is tired and I'm sure Nan is no doubt wondering what happened to us." She scrubbed at her face. "I don't want her to worry. She hasn't been herself lately."

"Nan is fine. She's with Dad and she's probably in better shape than most of us. Avery, please…let me help."

She shook her head. "I don't want to discuss this anymore. It's too much. I need to focus on one thing at a time. Right now that's taking care of Quinn. This discussion can wait until later."

"I agree," Grayson said as he opened the truck door for her. "We can talk more tomorrow."

She had one foot on the truck running board so when she shifted in his direction, they were at eye level.

He gave her a soft and sympathetic look, then closed the door as she sat down. Whatever her reasoning, or lack thereof, she was relieved when they finally pulled up to the Stone farm. The sun was just beginning to sink over the western horizon and there were lights in almost every window of the rambling farmhouse. Tucker's truck was parked close to the house.

"Why don't I carry Quinn inside," Grayson said as he got out. "Can you make it okay?"

"Of course," she assured him. "We really could have stayed at Nan's."

"No electricity with a well. That means no water."

He lifted their daughter from the backseat, then they walked together to the front door of the house. It opened as she reached for the handle.

"I've been so worried about you," Nan said as she gathered Avery up in a hug. Then her attention shifted to Quinn. "How is she feeling?"

"She's doing okay. She's tired, though. She slept most of the way home and she's had a headache," Avery told her foster mom. She didn't want to mention the house. If she did, she would cry again and she didn't want that.

Nan blinked and shook her head. "Of course she's tired. And I bet you are, too. Nina left food. She also made sure the extra beds have clean sheets. Let's get you both tucked in."

"I'm going to get Quinn tucked in and then I'll curl up on the sofa," Avery told her foster mom.

"There are plenty of rooms in this old house," Nan said, leading her inside, being overly gentle, as if she were an injured child. "I am so sorry about your house, honey. But you can start again."

"Yes, of course." Avery hugged her foster mother and didn't remind her that the contractor had left town. Why bring it up now?

Avery followed Grayson down the hall. The room he walked into was a small bedroom with a wrought iron bed, wicker dresser and white blinds on the windows. It wasn't fancy but it was cozy. Quinn smiled up at them as Grayson settled her in the bed. Avery stepped forward to cover her with a quilt that had been folded at the end of the bed. Quinn looked at them, her expression asking questions that Avery had no answers for.

"Will you sleep with me, Mom?" Quinn asked, her voice small and timid in a way that Avery hadn't expected.

"Of course, sweetie. Whatever you want. For now, I'll be in the living room, if you need me. Do you want water or something to eat?"

Quinn shook her head. "I'm not hungry, just tired."

Avery leaned to kiss her forehead. "Get some sleep."

"I will." Quinn waited until she was almost to the door. "Mom, I'm afraid of storms."

Avery slipped back into the room while Grayson left, giving them much needed time alone. Avery sank onto the bed and cuddled with her daughter, who suddenly seemed every bit the little girl she was.

"I know you're afraid. It's easy to be afraid when something like that happens. Then we think about it and worry about it too much. But remember my favorite verses…"

"Don't worry about tomorrow, today's troubles are sufficient for themselves. And we can't add a cubit to our stature by worrying."

"Right. Worry won't change anything," Avery reassured her daughter. "We can't stop storms, but we can pray and have faith. Yesterday could have been so much worse, honey. I'm so thankful that you're okay. Even the bad that happened can be fixed."

"Our house?"

"It might not be what we originally planned, but we will still build a home there."

She hugged Quinn tight and wished she could take away all of her fear, all of her pain.

"Mommy, I love you." Quinn's strong young arms wrapped around her neck.

"I love you more." She stood up from the bed and gave her daughter a last tender look. "I'll be in shortly."

She slipped from the room, knowing full well that Quinn would soon be asleep. Down the hall she found Grayson in the small but cozy living room.

"Is she okay?" he asked, moving to make room for her on the sofa.

"I think so. She's afraid and tired. I think the fear will take longer to heal than anything."

"I'm sure it will," Grayson agreed. "You hungry?"

"I am, a little."

He got up and pulled her to her feet. "Let's get a snack."

He led her to the country kitchen and opened the fridge.

"I know this is crazy, but I really want a fried bologna sandwich."

Ordinarily, she would have rejected such a thing but tonight it sounded just right. "I agree."

She stood, hip against the counter, watching as he expertly fried slices of bologna. Next, he buttered hamburger buns and grilled them with just a sprinkle of garlic. She giggled at him, at the entire process.

Grayson shot her a quick look as he forked the bologna onto the buns and then added a squirt of mustard. With flair, of course.

"What are you laughing at?" he asked as he handed over a plate with a sandwich and potato chips.

"You take your fried bologna very seriously."

"Cooking is an art," he informed her as he led her to the table in the attached dining room.

They sat next to each other eating their sandwiches, lost in thoughts about the past two days.

After finishing her sandwich, Avery sat back, trying to decide how she felt about this moment. For eleven years her feelings about Grayson had been…not so pleasant. And now here they sat, eating together, laughing together.

She was torn by how she felt about him. Still somewhat hurt and angry, not really trusting him, and yet, wanting him next to her.

Stuck between a rock and a hard place.

"We should get some sleep," Grayson said after a few minutes of sitting in companionable silence. Companionable, except for the changing expressions on Avery's face. If he had to guess, she was thinking too much. Doubting herself, doubting him.

He understood that, since he'd always had big doubts about himself. He wondered if it would help her to know that he'd spent his life—even his childhood, when he seemed so sure of himself—doubting his existence. He'd always doubted whether or not the judge wanted him in his home. He hadn't ever felt smart enough, good enough. He hadn't been enough for either of his parents.

He gathered up their plates from the table.

"I'll do the dishes." She took the plates from his hands.

"I can do the dishes."

Grayson smiled down at her, getting lost in the dark shadows under her eyes in the dimly lit room. He should have turned on more lights, made the room less dark. He paused to clear his thoughts and there she was, still looking up at him as if she, too, was trapped in this moment.

His younger self would have taken advantage of the moment. But he knew that no good could be found down this path. They hovered like that, on a precipice of emotion, tangled up in the past and the present.

Her eyes drifted closed for just a moment, then she let go of the plates and backed away. Good thing he still had hold of them. The crash would have woken up the whole house.

"I'll let you do the dishes." She spoke in hushed tones. "I should go check on Quinn anyway."

"Good night, Avery."

She hesitated, then spun around and hurried away from him. He watched her go, laughing unexpectedly. They were on a fast train, he and Avery. Maybe different trains.

Would they switch tracks, collide or figure out a way to be together as a family? He shook off the thoughts. He'd never been a romantic or a man given to poetry. And that sentiment was just a little too flowery for him.

He finished washing the dishes, stacked them in the drainer and went to check on Quinn. He stood motionless at the closed door, remembering that Avery had promised to sleep with their daughter. He wandered back to the living room. Nan was there.

"Nan, can I help you find something?"

She looked confused, as if she was sleepwalking.

"Grayson, what are you doing here?" she asked.

"Avery and I got home earlier, remember?"

Nan blinked a few times. "Oh, that's right. I think I was sleeping too hard and completely forgot where I was. I'm used to being at my old house. You know, I've only slept away from that place maybe a half dozen times in my entire life."

"No vacations, Nan?"

She sat down in his dad's beat-up old recliner that still smelled of cigar smoke, although the judge had quit smoking years ago. Why he didn't throw that chair out was a mystery.

"No, only a time or two to visit Avery and Quinn when they lived in Kansas City."

"Maybe you'll come visit me in California?" He asked as he sat down in the chair opposite hers.

She cocked her head to the side and studied him for a long moment. "Grayson, are you taking my girls from me?"

"I don't think they would go," he admitted. "Avery is past the stage of wanting me in her life. And I'll be honest, Nan. I'm scared to death of being the wrong man for her. I've hurt her before and I can't promise I wouldn't hurt her again."

"Oh, land's sakes, at some point you have to trust yourself and trust God."

"I do, most of the time. But I'm a recovering addict. I haven't felt a need to use in years, but that doesn't mean that I might not at some point."

She leaned forward in the chair. "Maybe so, Grayson. But maybe not. What if you miss out, all because of fear?"

"I would hate to miss out," he admitted.

She pushed herself out of the chair, still spry but moving a little slower tonight. Springing up, he gave her his arm and she took it, letting him guide her down the hallway to her room. She hesitated at Quinn's room.

"Do you want to check on them?" he asked.

"No, I'll let them sleep." She patted his arm and then she slipped into her room.

Grayson woke up several times during the night. As tired has he'd been, he had trouble falling and staying asleep.

At sunrise he gave up. He got up, dressed and went to sit on the covered back porch. He'd gotten into a habit of morning coffee and prayer time on that porch overlooking the Stone family farm. He enjoyed watching the distant traces of mist rising from the river. He even enjoyed watching the "livestock" as they grazed. Dolly, Jack and Tony the llama were forever a part of this place. Even if they did get out on an almost daily basis. It wasn't that he didn't repair the fences; it was just that they always found a new place to escape.

The cattle also grazed but their presence wasn't quite the same. Somehow, he'd gotten attached to the misfit animals his father had brought home.

His attention turned to the building site across the way. The frame of the house gone, it now looked like someone had played a game of pick up sticks. Avery had planned that home for herself and her daughter. She would continue to live with Nan, but that didn't ease the heartache of her loss. This morning there would be families all over the area waking up in a new reality.

Their homes or businesses were gone, their barns were gone, livestock also gone.

As he walked across the rain-damp grass in the direction of the barn, he knew that he could and would help. Pleasant had been his hometown, the place where he grew up. He was here now for a purpose. He thought back to his original plan to come here for a weeklong trip, not weeks. If things hadn't changed, he wouldn't have been here with Avery, with Quinn, helping his community, building these relationships.

Tony the llama came to the fence for his morning pat on the head. That was all Tony wanted. He wasn't a particularly affectionate animal. Jack the donkey liked to have his ears rubbed. Dolly the miniature horse was all about the attention. She rubbed against the fence post, waiting for him to scratch her back, her neck, her ears.

"Give me a minute and I'll feed you," he assured the pint-size horse. She whinnied as if she understood him, then she trotted along the fence toward the barn. He had feed buckets for each of them and sometimes they kept to their own feed. Usually, they didn't. In the field to the north of the house, the cattle had spotted him and they were moving toward the trough where he poured the bags of grain each morning.

"Nice livestock." Avery's voice came from the front of the barn as he loaded the grain into the wheelbarrow.

"Unique livestock," he answered without turning. "How are you this morning?"

"I'm good. Thank you for taking such good care of us."

He spun the wheelbarrow to face her. "Did you get any sleep?"

Her mouth hitched up on one side and her green eyes drew him in. "A little. How about you?"

"I don't require a lot of sleep. How's Quinn?"

"Still sleeping. I had to get up and call work. They're moving most of our residents to other facilities."

"What does that mean for you?"

"I'll have a job, for now. I'm not sure if they'll close the center or try to make repairs." She walked with him as he pushed the wheelbarrow through the gate and into the field. "Maybe all of this happened for a reason. I mean, the contractor took my money but maybe it stopped me from getting further into debt when I was about to lose my job."

"I don't think you should go to worst-case scenario just yet. If you don't have this job, I know you can get another."

"Right, but maybe not this close to home. I like working in the same town my daughter lives in and goes to school in."

"I know, but things don't always go according to plan. But that doesn't mean God doesn't have a plan or that everything will fall apart."

"I'm not sure if I can have this conversation with you right now," she told him, stopping a short distance from the milling cattle and watching as he poured the grain into the trough.

He paused, watching her for a moment. She stood in the knee-deep emerald grass, grass that was nearly the color of her eyes. The blades of grass swayed in the wind.

"Why not?" He averted his gaze, watching the cattle because cattle were less complicated than this situation. "We share a daughter. Like it or not, we're in each other's lives. There will be graduations, dances, college, a wedding. Why not share our troubles, our fears, or even our dreams?"

"I know all of that. I do. It's just a lot, to have these conversations but also—" she moved her hands "—you are not usually the person who discusses faith and God. Not that I know anything about you. I knew a boy and you're no longer that boy."

"You're right, I'm not that person anymore, Avery," he stated. "I've learned a better way to live."

"I'm glad," she said after a long pause. "I am happy for you."

He was, too. "I appreciate that. I'm going to be honest. Being back home has made me doubt myself."

"Doubt yourself?"

He'd started the conversation, now he wished he could take it back. "In California, I know myself. I know the person I've become. Here, I'm back to being the renegade Stone boy. I also just recently learned I have a daughter." He smiled at that. "And I don't want to let her down."

"I don't want you to let her down," she agreed with an honesty that shook him a little.

"Let's go take a look at your house," he suggested.

"You mean, what's left of my house."

He pushed the wheelbarrow back to the barn. "No, I mean, your house. I'm going to make sure this works out for you." Before he left, he would make sure his daughter and her mother had a home or at least the start of a home.

He waited for her to object. She didn't. Instead she followed him into the barn, waited for him to put everything back in order, and then walked next to him as they started for her piece of property.

"This is difficult for me," she said a few minutes into their walk.

He wasn't sure which "this" she referred to so he gave her a look and waited for her to answer.

"Letting you help me. I'm pretty independent, in case you haven't noticed."

"Oh, I've noticed. Thank you for trusting me enough to let me help. It means a lot to me, to know that I've contributed. She's my daughter, Avery. I want to be more than a guy who shows up to visit once or twice a year."

More silence between them. They were nearing the building site, now a place of scattered debris. Avery's indrawn breath reflected the look of disbelief as she studied the scene. He reached for her hand and she slid her fingers through his.

"Yesterday I convinced myself it was a dream, a bad dream. Today is the reality." She slipped through the barbed wire as he held it up for her. After she was through, she pulled up the loose strand and he joined her on the other side.

As they approached what had been a home in progress, a tear slid down her cheek. She swiped it away.

"This hurts," she said.

"I know." He had released her hand but he reached for it once more.

Together they walked around the area, picking up the boards that had scattered in the storm.

"I guess this is all trash now?" she asked.

He looked at the boards he'd picked up and stacked to one side of the foundation.

"We can reuse some of this. It's blown apart but the boards are still in one piece, most of them. Some of this..." He picked up a two-by-four and shook his head. "I think your builder was cutting more corners than you realized."

"Really?" she asked as she looked at the pile they'd made.

"Really. Trust me, this is something I know about."

She nodded, agreeing. She was beautiful. She always had been but he found the woman even more attractive than the teenager he'd known. She knew herself better and maybe that was the difference. This morning her blond hair had been tied back with a blue ribbon. He realized she'd changed clothes from yesterday's outfit. She wore a T-shirt and sweatpants.

"Are those my clothes?" he asked.

"I didn't have anything." Her face grew pink and she glanced away, peering across the field they'd just crossed. "Quinn is coming."

"Good thing."

"Why?" she asked as if she didn't already know.

"Because I really wanted to kiss you."

She put several feet between them as her cheeks turned pink. "Grayson, you're too much for me. You always have been. And I haven't ever been enough for you. We have to think about Quinn. I won't let her build daydreams about you in our lives, or about us together."

He wanted to disagree but quickly he realized the wisdom in her words. She was right to keep a distance between them. He'd always hurt her and he would hurt her again. This time there was Quinn to consider.

He pasted on a fake smile and turned to greet their daughter. From that moment on, as much as he wanted to spend more time with Avery, he had to remember that he was here for Quinn.

Just Quinn.

Chapter Nine

"We're going to be late," Nan chided on Sunday morning. It had been four days since the tornado had ripped through their community.

Avery didn't want to remind Nan that they were running late because Nan couldn't find her slow cooker, only to realize it had already been put in the car, along with cookies, pies and a casserole. The church was serving lunch to the workers who had been tirelessly helping to clean up the town from the tornado, and to local families who were still displaced or living without electricity.

Avery zoomed the car into a parking space, ignoring the looks given to her by both Nan and Quinn. "Made it," she said cheekily as she hopped out and started to unload all of the food Nan had made.

"Late," Nan said. "But at least we made it."

"We aren't late. The bell is just now ringing," Avery defended.

"When Nan says we made it, I think she means safely." Quinn danced out of her reach. "That one corner you took on two wheels? That was awesome."

"Stop. You know I didn't—"

Then Avery saw him. He headed their way, all smooth confidence and charm. She ignored the desire to take a longer look. He was just a man. A man in jeans and a button-up shirt and those "all hat and no cattle" boots of his. Today he wore an expensive-looking white Western hat that settled low over his dark hair, dark with just a hint of auburn. Just like Quinn's.

Quinn hurried to join him, leaving Avery and Nan to watch as she greeted her father.

Nan whistled.

"That's inappropriate," Avery whispered.

Nan laughed a little. "So is that look on your face, but I didn't mention that, now, did I?"

Avery ignored her. Grayson and Quinn were nearly to them and no way would he not notice the telltale sign of embarrassment that had obviously crawled into her too-fair cheeks.

"I thought maybe you weren't coming to church today," Grayson said as he joined them. He smiled at his daughter. "How are you feeling this morning?"

Quinn reacted by giving him a hug. "I'm good. No more headache."

"I'm glad you're feeling better."

The way his face changed when he looked at Quinn did something to Avery that his mere looks couldn't. It undid a little bit of her heart, making room for the man who was her daughter's father.

As much as she'd always denied it, Quinn needed him. "Could you help us get the food inside?" Avery asked, pushing the slow cooker into his hands.

"Sure thing," he said with a grin.

She also stuck the handle of a bag in his hand.

"Can you get all of that?"

Their gazes met, and for a brief second she wished he hadn't caught up with them. A few minutes later he would have been inside and she wouldn't have to deal with all of the things he made her feel. Insecure, afraid, grounded. He made her feel safe, too. She should feel the opposite of safe with him. He was anything but.

Nan grabbed a tray of cookies out of the back and handed them to Quinn, then picked up a casserole dish. "Quinn and I are going on in."

"But…" Quinn started. She glanced back at them as Nan gave her a bit of a nudge. "I thought we would…"

"Nope," Nan told her. "We need to get this stuff inside."

Avery watched them leave. Unfortunately, Nan was not subtle. Ever.

"That wasn't too obvious, was it?" Grayson asked, trying to tamp down a grin on his face.

"Not too much. Grayson, I don't think we should sit together."

"What?" He stopped short, and she stood next to him. People were entering the church, some through the front doors and some through the side. Those same people were staring, wondering what sort of drama she'd gotten herself into now.

Not that most of them didn't know what was going on. The entire town knew that Grayson had returned and she was sure most of them knew that he was Quinn's dad. They'd probably always known but were just too nice to say it to her face.

"Why can't we sit together?" he asked too loudly. She cringed.

"Shhh, keep it down."

"Why can't we sit together, Avery? Every time I think I've figured this—us—out, you change directions on me."

"I don't mean to. This situation isn't something I planned for and I don't know the rules."

"It isn't exactly what I was prepared for, either, so we're even. But I do need an explanation for why you don't want me to sit with you."

"Quinn. I don't want her to get the wrong idea. I don't want her to think we're a family. Every Sunday we are in church, and it's the two of us and Nan. All around her are families that look different than hers. Families with a mom, dad, siblings, grandparents. I know this sounds irrational but just try to understand."

"So you're saying you're afraid she'll get her hopes up if I sit with you at church."

She nodded, hoping he would understand. From the way he shook his head, she guessed he didn't.

"Nope, not buying it. I think you want to protect yourself, not our daughter. We're a family, Avery. We might not look like the other families, but this is what we have, what Quinn has. She has a mom, a dad and she has grandparents. My dad. Nan. Those are her grand-parents."

She bristled at his calm tone and knowing words. He'd only just found out he had a daughter and already he was the expert on parenting?

The worst part was, he was right.

"Stop," he said quietly as he stepped closer.

"Stop what?"

"Overthinking. This is our situation. We can't change it or go back so we move forward and make it work."

"Right, you're right." She looked down at the dish

in her hands. They'd been standing outside the church for a while. The bell had stopped ringing. People were no longer going inside. "We have to get this food to the kitchen."

"Yes, we're already late."

They hurried together to fellowship hall where lunch would be served immediately after church. It took a little work to find a place for the dishes they'd brought. The counters were already covered with slow cookers, casseroles and desserts. Several women were making sure everything was ready to be served.

One of the ladies took charge of their dishes and told them to scoot. On their way out the door she called out to them.

"By the way, you two look real happy together," Miss Lana said. She'd been a Sunday school teacher at church and worked in the cafeteria at school. She'd known them both forever.

Avery felt her cheeks heat up as she kept walking while Grayson stopped to thank her.

They hurried through the church to the sanctuary. As they entered, the announcements were being read. Avery scanned the crowd and spotted Nan sitting next to Mathias Stone, with Quinn next to her.

"Forgive me," Grayson whispered in her ear as they stood in the entrance to the sanctuary.

A few people craned their heads to see who was standing next to Avery. Mouths began to move as people talked. Or mostly gossiped. Gossip really didn't have a place in church.

"Forgive you?" she asked, confused because her mind had wandered.

"I wasn't a friend to you. I know I'm much too late

but I'd like your forgiveness. And I hope we can be friends as we raise Quinn."

The words shook her because he'd said them before. Not as eloquently. He'd been a teenager and he'd told her they were friends. But when she'd truly needed his friendship, he hadn't been there for her. When she'd been nineteen and pregnant, he'd been long gone with no way to find him. Words had always been easy for Grayson Stone. The actions to back up the words were a different story.

Trust didn't come easily for her, not just because of Grayson but because of a lifetime of people who had let her down. Could she forgive him?

"Avery, this is the adult me asking you to forgive the teenage me."

She nodded. "I know, and I'm working on it. I do forgive you. But I'm doing so with boundaries."

"Understood." He inclined his head toward the pew where Nan and Quinn waited. "Shall we do this? Together. I'm not as brave as I look."

Somehow, she gathered herself up, put on a cloak of bravery, picked up her faith and took a seat in that church pew with Grayson Stone at her side.

The church fellowship hall was packed with members and visitors as they served up a huge meal for workers who had converged upon the community of Pleasant and the outlying area. Workers from the electric company, tree service workers and volunteers from other churches were all lined up together, as well as people who'd experienced damage to their homes. They were filling their plates and talking about things other than the storm.

Grayson got it. People wanted to get back to their normal lives. They wanted, even just for a short time, to think about something other than lost homes and the daunting task of rebuilding.

He stood next to Pastor Wilson discussing the damage to the church youth building. But Grayson's attention started wandering to Avery. She was standing behind the tables laden with food, laughing at something the lady next to her had said, then served another helping of potatoes to the next person in line. She greeted the elderly man with a soft smile and leaned a little to hear what he said in response.

"What's your plan?"

"I'm sorry?" Grayson jerked his attention back to the pastor. "I didn't catch what you said."

Pastor Wilson laughed. "I know you didn't. I asked about your plan."

"I'm making sure my dad is settled before I go back to California." His gaze drifted once again to Avery.

Her soft laughter carried across the room and she lit up as she and the pastor's wife discussed something with a woman Grayson didn't recognize.

"I hadn't really meant your plan regarding your father," Pastor Wilson said. The man was nothing if not tenacious.

"I'm not sure," Grayson answered. "For now I'm just trying to get to know my daughter."

"I see," Pastor Wilson said. He didn't sound impressed by Grayson's answer.

"Dad, are you going to eat with us?" A hand tugged on Grayson's arm, and it took him a moment to realize he was the dad. Quinn beamed up at him. Behind her stood three girls of similar age.

"With you?" he teased.

"Yes." She grinned. "And Nan and Grandpa Judge."

"Grandpa Judge?" That was a new one.

She giggled. "Yeah. He was a judge and he's my grandpa. Also, when I call him Grandpa Judge he growls but then he smiles."

"I'll join you in a minute," he promised. "What about your mom?"

"She's coming in a minute, too. She's still serving food."

And avoiding him, if he had to guess.

Quinn walked away, her friends tagging along with her. Grayson ignored the look Pastor Wilson gave him. An expectant look, one that felt like an exclamation mark on their previous conversation about his plans for the future.

"I'm going to stop by tomorrow to look at the youth building and to write up a supply list for the repairs," Grayson said, shifting the conversation to one that felt less restrictive. He could breathe if he was discussing building.

"I'll be here by eight o'clock," Pastor Wilson said. "I'll have a couple of our men here, in case we need to get approval for the expenses."

"We won't worry about that for right now," Grayson said. "I grew up in this church and I'd like to be able to help with the cost of repairing the youth building. Tucker told me what you all have been doing here, feeding kids, making sure they have clothes for school, coats for the winter. I want to be able to do my part in your ministry."

"We appreciate that." Pastor Wilson held out a hand to him.

"Did I hear my name mentioned?" Tucker joined them. A girl stood at his side. If Grayson had to guess, she looked to be in her early teens. She didn't seem very happy about being there with him.

"This must be your niece." Grayson smiled down at the girl.

She didn't smile back. Tucker gave her a slight nudge.

"Shay, this is my friend Grayson Stone. We went to school together."

"Hi, Shay, nice to meet you." Grayson tried again, holding his hand out to the girl.

She looked at his hand for a brief moment, then ignored him. Tucker looked more than a little beside himself. It did Grayson a little bit of good to see that he wasn't the only one struggling with the women in his life.

"I need to join my family," Grayson said. "Tucker, would you and Shay like to join us? Pastor, you're invited, too, if you think you can handle it." He winked at him.

Pastor Wilson laughed. "I have four daughters. I'm not afraid. But I'm going to circulate and talk to people. We're still trying to make a list of things that need to be done, church members and neighbors who might need help with repairs or cleanup. I'm taking some of our youth out Tuesday afternoon to help clean up trash. Shay is welcome to come with us."

"No, thanks," Shay quickly replied.

Tucker cut her off. "She'll be here, just tell me what time."

Avery happened to be passing by, and she stopped to join their conversation. "I'd like to be a part of that group, too, Pastor. I won't be working at PRC for a few days so I might as well help you all."

The residential facility had unfortunately suffered more damage than it first appeared. Grayson knew that Avery was worried for her job but also the residents who had been displaced.

"I'll help with that, too." Grayson said, smiling at Avery.

"Well, this should be downright fun," Tucker said. "Shay and I wouldn't miss it for the world."

Avery laughed and walked away. Grayson watched her go and didn't follow. He needed a moment because he was quickly realizing he might be in over his head. He couldn't be partially involved with his daughter, and it was becoming clearer by the moment that he wanted to be more than partially in Avery's life. He wanted it all.

The thought left him shaken.

Chapter Ten

Tuesday afternoon Grayson watched as Avery worked tirelessly helping the Atkins family clean up the debris that littered their yard. The family had lost part of their roof, their back porch and several trees on their property.

Along with several other women, Avery carried trash and small limbs. They laughed together as they worked, occasionally stopping to talk.

He started moving in her direction, picking up boards as he went and tossing them in the Dumpster that had been brought in for the cleanup.

Tucker caught up with him when he was a short distance away from Avery. "How's it going?"

"Going well."

"Is it?" Tucker asked, his gaze straying to Avery.

"Do you have something to say, Church?"

Tucker just grinned. "Nah, I'm just messing with you, man. But I did want to touch base about the thing we talked about? I can deliver it soon."

Grayson kept one eye on Avery. "That would be good. In the next couple of days would be perfect."

"Are they still staying at the farm?"

"Yes, for now. It looks like power will be back on at Nan's place in the next couple of days but until then, they're with us."

Tucker picked up a section of roofing and heaved it into the Dumpster with the other debris. "What about the house?"

"Avery's house?" Grayson asked, just to clarify.

"Yeah."

They moved over to one side as a man walked past with an extension ladder. All around them were groups of people helping to get things taken care of. A couple of men were working on the roof, dragging a tarp over an area that was damaged.

"I've been working over there in the evenings. I want to get as much done as possible before I have to leave. I'm putting together crews for plumbing, drywall, electric."

"She doesn't mind your help?" Tucker asked as he pulled his gloves back on.

"She might mind just a little." He shrugged. "This tornado changed everything, though."

"When do you plan on leaving?" Tucker asked.

The man had a dozen questions.

"End of June or beginning of July. I'm not really sure yet. I'm thinking about asking Avery to take care of the judge. She knows how to handle him."

"I think Avery has her hands full with Quinn, Nan and a full-time job."

"It's not clear what's going to happen with PRC. They're talking about closing it down. The damage to the place was more extensive than they'd first thought.

They've moved a big percentage of residents to other facilities."

Across the yard, Grayson noticed Avery had paused to brush hair from her face. Quinn joined her as they picked up paper, insulation and other scraps. Both wore gloves and masks. Quinn looked the slightest bit pale.

"I'm going to check on Quinn," Grayson said as he took a few steps away from Tucker. "It might be time to take her home."

"She does look like she's about done in," Tucker agreed. "If I haven't said it, I think you're good for her."

"I appreciate that," Grayson answered. And he did. "See you later. We still have to take that float trip."

"I agree. See you in a couple of days with that special delivery."

Grayson raised a hand to acknowledge what Tucker had said as he walked away, smiling at the idea of the surprise, the special delivery Tucker had mentioned. Quinn would have her dream. He couldn't give her everything but he could do this one thing.

Avery gave him a sharp look as he approached.

"How're you doing?" he asked.

"Great. I'm doing great," she answered as she walked away to dump an armload of trash in the Dumpster. He followed close behind.

"Quinn looks tired," he said.

Avery gave her daughter, *their* daughter, a quick look. "She does look pale. I'll have her take a break in the shade."

"I have water in my truck. I can get her a bottle. You want one, too?"

Avery pulled off the leather work gloves she wore

and swiped a hand across her face. "I wouldn't say no to some cold water right now."

Grayson headed to his truck. He glanced back once and saw Avery talking to Quinn. Quinn didn't look happy, but she seemed to be doing what Avery asked. She headed to a tree where there was shade and she sank to the ground to rest.

As he reached into the back of his truck cab to pull a couple of bottles of water from the cooler, a voice rang out behind him. "Grayson Stone, it's mighty strange to see you in this neck of the woods."

Slowly, he turned, knowing who he would see standing behind him. "Greg Butterfield, it's been a long time."

"Yeah, it has. Eleven years. One minute we were wild and crazy and then you were gone." Greg's eyes darted around the area. They were pretty well isolated. "Been a long time since we partied together."

"Yeah, well, I quit partying a long time ago," Grayson admitted. "Do you attend the community church?"

Greg laughed at that. "Nah, this is my cousin's place and I told him I'd help him out. I can help you out, too."

Grayson knew exactly what he was hinting at. "I don't think so, Greg. Clean and sober for nine years. I plan on keeping it that way."

"Does that mean you can't hang out with an old friend?" Greg asked.

He held up the bottles of water. "I have to deliver these."

"Oh, that's right, to your wifey and your kid." Greg's eyes narrowed. "Avery grew up to be real pretty, didn't she?"

Grayson studied the other man, wondering if that was a threat or an observation. Either way, it bothered him.

"Stay away from her," Grayson warned.

The other man cackled. "Oh, come on, Grayson, we're old friends."

"See you around, Greg." Grayson walked away. From across the lawn he made eye contact with Avery. She'd seen them talking. Even from a distance he knew there would be a flicker of doubt in her green eyes. Well-deserved doubt. He even doubted himself.

That was the problem with being in a small town where everyone knew you. There was no way he could be in Pleasant and not bump into his old buddies. Not that any of them had been friends.

"Water for my girls," he said when he reached Avery and Quinn. He handed Quinn a bottle, twisting the lid off before giving it to her. Avery gave him the stink eye, probably for referring to her as "his girl."

"We're going home," Avery told him. "I mean, to your house. Quinn has a headache and it's almost dinnertime. I'm pretty sure Nan said something about making homemade chicken pot pie for dinner."

"We should definitely go," Quinn said, more inclined to leave than he would have thought.

He and Avery had brought separate cars so they weren't going to leave together. It unsettled him, their sudden departure. Maybe because he'd bumped into Greg, he realized. He'd come face-to-face with his sketchy past and he hadn't enjoyed it.

"I think I'll leave, too." He reached out for his daughter and she slipped her small hand into his. Pulling her up to stand, he said, "Maybe Nan made dessert to go with the chicken pot pie."

"Oh, I hope so." Quinn grinned at him.

* * *

Avery drove home by herself. Quinn had opted to ride with her father. It hadn't been easy, letting go, but Avery had done it. For Quinn and Grayson both. Still, it hurt the tiniest bit that Quinn had picked him over her.

Being alone gave Avery time to think about the conversation she'd witnessed between Greg and Grayson. The two men had been friends as teens. They had partied together, gotten in trouble together and probably would have ended up the same if Grayson's parents hadn't sent him away.

Seeing them together reminded her too much of the past. Of who he used to be, and she knew that wasn't fair. People changed.

With her thoughts swirling around in her head, Avery was surprised when a small horse ran in front of her car. She slammed on the brakes, her heart nearly jumping out of her chest. Dolly raced off down the driveway, Jack the donkey close behind her.

Avery pulled over to the side of the driveway and got out.

Grayson's truck came up the driveway behind her and pulled to a stop. He and Quinn got out and Quinn whistled shrilly, bringing the two escapees to a sudden stop.

"Wow, where did you learn to whistle like that?" Grayson asked.

"Grandpa Judge taught me," Quinn said as she moved finger and thumb to her mouth and whistled again to show him.

"That's pretty impressive," Grayson told her. "I'm going to have to learn to do that."

Then the conversation came to a halt. The donkey

and horse were on the run again. Quinn went after them, running on the opposite side of the drive.

"Circle around them," Grayson yelled, chasing after her. "We'll divide and conquer."

Father and daughter were both laughing and yelling as they tried to corner the two animals. Dolly, with her reddish-brown coat and black mane, streaked past her two would-be captors. She shook her head in victory as she tried to make a run for it.

Quinn hurried to catch up with her as Jack the donkey cut in the other direction and tried to slide past Grayson. More shouting and some slipping and sliding in the gravel. Cowboy boots were not meant for running on gravel roads.

Jack darted past them, his tail swishing as he ran. Then out of nowhere, the basset hound came to join the chase.

"That beast," Grayson called out, laughing as he went after Jack. The basset followed, his hound dog bark not really helping.

Tony the llama had found a way out of his enclosure, but uninterested in running, he began to graze. He would occasionally raise his head and watch the flight of Jack, chewing with blades of grass sticking out of the corner of his mouth. His eyes were brown, fringed with long lashes. He looked very sweet. Avery approached the animal only to have him bellow and then spit.

She held her hands up in surrender and backed away. The donkey and horse were still leading Grayson and Quinn on a merry chase. Avery headed for the barn. She scooped up a bucket of grain and walked back to the yard, shaking the pail as she went. Tony the llama immediately returned to the yard. Farther down the drive, Jack and Dolly came to a halt. Jack's antenna-like ears swiveled, and he made an abrupt 180 degree turn and headed back to the barn. Dolly nuzzled up against Quinn, as if that had always been her plan.

Avery kept shaking the bucket of food and headed for the corral that would hopefully keep them confined this time. She opened the gate and walked through the opening. A moment later Tony, Jack and Dolly had followed her inside. She poured the grain in a wooden trough, then hurried back through the gate.

Grayson closed it behind her and latched it. "I'm not sure why he thought he needed those animals. They're more trouble than they're worth."

Quinn giggled. "I love them."

"And *that's* why we won't get rid of them," Grayson acknowledged as he leaned against the fence, trying to catch his breath. "Thanks for the help. You were amazing."

Quinn arched a brow at that. "My mom is the one who really got them in."

"I'm just the one who had the grain," Avery said. "The two of you did all the hard work."

"We're a good team," Grayson said.

Quinn had a funny look on her face as her gaze slid from Grayson to Avery. She studied them.

"It's like we're a family," she said after a minute.

This had been Avery's greatest fear, that Quinn would want more. And she didn't blame her. Avery had spent her entire childhood wanting two parents who would be there for her, be present in her life. She'd done her very best to give Quinn one parent who would be those things and who wouldn't let her down.

Grayson was larger than life to a ten-year-old who

longed for a family that was more than a mom and grandmother. Avery understood that. From the first time they'd met, he'd always been larger than life to her, as well.

"That donkey bit me," Grayson said, very out of the blue.

He held his hand out. Avery peered at the spot he was pointing to and she exhaled a breath, relaxing. She tossed him a look, silently thanking him for the distraction.

"That isn't a bite. It looks like…" Avery looked up to meet his gaze. "It looks like he might have licked your hand."

Grayson glanced at the indention. "I beg to differ. It is a bite. He could have taken my finger off."

"If that was his goal, he should try harder." She reached through the wooden fence to pet the donkey. The rascal ducked his head to nip at her leg. "That was just a friendship bite. He didn't even use his teeth."

"I'm going up to the house to see Grandpa Judge," Quinn told them.

Grayson and Avery remained at the corral, watching their daughter as she hurried to the house.

"Can I tell you a secret?" he asked.

"Sure," she said, though not entirely convinced she wanted to know.

He didn't answer right away, then said, "Parenting is frightening."

She arched a brow at the statement. "Truly frightening," she agreed.

"Suddenly, there are cars and strangers and hidden dangers that she has to be kept safe from."

"And boys who think she's cute."

"Right, boys." He gave a heavy sigh.

"It gets easier, I promise," she encouraged.

"I know it does, but it's a lot. Two weeks ago I was Grayson Stone, builder, single man, passing through his hometown to check on his dad."

"Now?"

"I'm a dad. And there is no *passing through* my child's life."

Her heart gave a painful squeeze and she blinked away tears that gathered. He might be larger than life but he was also thoughtful in ways that mattered. That was the new Grayson, not the one she'd known a dozen years ago.

"I didn't mean to make you cry." He squeezed her hand.

Avery shook her head in denial that she was crying but swiped at a tear that trickled down her cheek.

"I'm glad you aren't passing through her life." Her own father had done that to her and she'd vowed she'd never allow that to happen to her daughter.

The thoughts brought her to a stop, guilt and shame flooding her.

"Avery? What's wrong?"

"I let my fear do this to you and to Quinn."

"Your fear?"

"Grayson, I have to protect Quinn. I won't let her live the life I lived. I don't want her to feel the heartache of being neglected or abandoned. I don't want her to be anything other than confident and sure of herself. My father walked out shortly after I was born. He never came back. I don't know where he went, maybe a new life, maybe jail. But I didn't search for him, either. I know his name. I know I have a grandmother in

Illinois. I never went looking for either of them. They didn't want me so why should I want them?"

"So...you're saying I paid for your father's sins?"

"Yes, yes, you did." She stood there quietly, feeling the tears sliding down her face. "Please forgive me, Grayson," she whispered.

"I forgive you," he answered. "I understand but wow, I just don't know how to process all of this. You're telling me I missed ten years of Quinn's life because of another man's actions?"

"I know."

"I want to make sure you know that I won't miss another birthday, another Christmas, another year. I'm not sure what God's plans are with all of this, but I do know that none of this was an accident."

"I see."

"Do you?" he asked. "God knew that I had a daughter here. She was never a secret to Him. And God knew that it was time to end this cycle. You deserved a father, Avery. And my daughter deserves to have me in her life, as a father and not as a visitor."

Avery squeezed her eyes shut tight and allowed her heart to open up just a little. Quinn needed her father. She needed this man who promised to be there for her.

She prayed hard that he would keep those promises.

Grayson put his arm around Avery. "Let's go back and see if Nan needs help with dinner."

They walked back from the corral, then entered the house to find the kitchen dark.

"Nan?" Avery called out, heading from the back of the house to the front.

"She isn't here," Nina answered from the laundry room. The caretaker came out, a pile of folded towels in her arms. "She went to her house to work on a boat. She said she has an order and she can't just stop working. I tried to get her to stay here but she was stubborn."

"There's still no electricity at the house." Avery reached for the purse she'd dropped on the counter as she came in. "Why would she go work on a boat when she really can't do any? Where is Mr. Stone?"

"He's on the front porch," Nina said with a smirk. "He might have been watching the show as you all tried to catch the runaways."

"I'm going to sell those animals first thing tomorrow." Grayson issued the empty warning with a grin.

"No, you won't." Avery knew that with a certainty. "Is Quinn with him?"

"She is," Nina said.

"I'm going to check on Nan," Avery said as she headed for the back door. "Is it okay if Quinn stays here? She really does need to rest."

"Of course she can stay here," Nina answered as she carried towels into the bathroom.

"I'll go," Grayson broke in. "I'll check on Nan. You stay here and make sure Quinn rests."

The sound of a vehicle rumbling up the drive stopped their conversation. Grayson went to the kitchen window. "Nan's back."

"Good." Avery went out the back door. Quinn started to follow but Grayson told her to wait. She mouthed a quiet "Thank you." She needed a moment alone with her foster mom, to make sure she was okay.

Nan met her in the yard and she certainly looked well enough.

"Nina said you went home to work on your boat,"

Avery said, trying to sound fairly normal, not at all concerned.

"That was my plan. But I got there and there was no electricity. I'm not sure why I thought it would be back on today. And then it took me a little longer than expected to get back here."

"Oh, why was that?"

Nan shrugged off the question. "It's a pretty day for a drive."

"Yes, it is." Avery walked with her foster mom, back to the house and into the kitchen where the others waited.

"Oh dear, I forgot to make chicken pot pie." Nan sighed. "This storm has me rattled. I have an idea. Why don't we send Grayson to town for fish dinners from Tilly's?"

"We could make sandwiches," Avery suggested.

"I think fish dinners are a great idea," Grayson said as he gave Nan a hug. "I love Tilly's fish."

"Me, too." Nan patted his cheek. "You're not so bad."

"You're pretty terrific yourself," he told her.

Avery walked Grayson to his truck. "Are you sure you don't mind doing this? I feel as if we've become the worst kind of houseguest, the kind that doesn't leave and now you're having to feed us."

"You're the best houseguest and I don't mind at all. And stop worrying. I think Nan is fine."

"I hope so. She hasn't been herself lately."

"She made a valid point. This storm has rattled all of us. Give her a week or so to get past it and I'm sure she'll be back to her usual self."

"Thank you," Avery said as they stopped next to his truck.

"Thank you for what?"

She touched his cheek. "For being here. For being thoughtful. For giving us a place to stay."

"I think I was here at the right time, Avery."

"Maybe so," she agreed.

"I'll be back with dinner." He leaned down, catching her mouth in a warm kiss that took her by surprise, not only because it was unexpected but also because it shifted the foundation of her world.

He broke the kiss off and got in his truck, leaving her a bit dazed as she watched him drive away.

Boundaries, she reminded herself. She really needed to remember those boundaries. Grayson was easy to look at, easy to kiss. He always had been. It was all of the other stuff that got in the way. No matter how much she wanted to trust him, she kept waiting for him to do or say something that would hurt her or her daughter.

Grayson slowed as he drove through Pleasant on his way to Tilly's. As he passed by the feed store, a man got out of a car to talk to someone in a truck. Grayson recognized both men. Once, a long time ago, they'd been friends. The worst kind of friends.

The man who had been sitting in the car turned to catch his eye. Recognition flared. Chet Martin waved at Grayson, wanting him to come over. He yelled something that Grayson didn't hear. Then a third car pulled in. Greg.

Some people changed. Some people didn't. For Grayson, there was always a fine line. A line he hadn't crossed in nine years. As he drove on past, he thought of Quinn. Of Avery. He thought about how easy it would be to let them down and how much he didn't want to be the person Avery couldn't count on.

Pleasant represented a past he didn't want to get tangled up in. Ever again.

Chapter Eleven

Avery went in to work at PRC on Thursday. It had been eight days since the tornado hit Pleasant and the surrounding area. For six of those days they'd stayed at the Stone farm. Going back home had felt good. Back to Nan's. Back to their routine and back to the security that Avery felt in that farmhouse.

It felt odd, to return to work, to note all of the differences. Three of the halls had been shut down. More than half of the residents had been evacuated to residential homes in the area. The small number of residents who remained were confined to their rooms. All those changes meant that a large portion of the staff had been let go or moved to other facilities.

Slipping into a darkened room, she took a seat next to the bed. Margie opened her eyes and smiled. "It's about time you showed up."

"I'm sorry," Avery whispered, and reached for Margie's hand. "I've missed you."

"I've missed you, as well. It's been very quiet here. How's Mr. All Hat and No Cattle?"

"Margie, Mr. All Hat is Grayson Stone. Do you remember him?"

"Well, of course I do. He's Judge Stone's boy. He was wild as a March hare, that one was. And you always were calf eyed when he was around."

"Calf eyed?"

"Big eyes watching that boy. Even when he was ornery to you."

"Yes, even when he was ornery." She thought about that for a minute. "He once told some kids that he couldn't invite me to a party. His mom didn't want trailer park trash in her house."

"That was unfair of him, but he was just a boy back then. He was probably trying to impress someone and didn't know how hurtful it was. Kids do that. But what about now?"

"He's Quinn's father," she confessed to the older woman. "What am I supposed to do?"

She didn't know why she was asking Margie. Maybe because she needed the impartial wisdom of this woman she had always admired?

"Ahhh, that makes sense. She has his dark hair and dark eyes. I'm guessing he didn't know."

"No, he didn't."

Margie patted her hand. "Oh, the tangled webs we weave, trying to hide our secrets and protect our hearts."

"It was a mistake," Avery admitted.

"Yes, it was. We all make them so don't be too hard on yourself."

Avery sighed. "I'm afraid it's too late for that."

"Now's the chance for the two of you to make up for the past."

Both of them had things to make up for, not just

Grayson. She had realized that but when Margie had put it into words, that made it hit home all the more.

"You're right. I know I can't give him the ten years he lost. It's tough."

"It is, but you'll do the right thing for them both. And for yourself. Trust in the Lord with all of your heart, Avery. It's the 'all' that matters."

"Thank you." She glanced at her watch. "I have to go now."

"Will you be back?" Margie's voice brightened. "I heard we're going to start our Bible study again. I thought we'd never get back to normal."

"The storm changed everything, didn't it?" Nothing had been normal since the storm.

"Life has its storms, Avery." Margie pushed the button to raise up the back of her bed. "I can't stand lying down like that. I need to be able to sit up and see you. I want you to remember that life has storms, but you remember Who is in the storm with you. And remember that storms never last forever."

"I'll remember." Avery stood, then leaned over to hug Margie. "I'm so thankful for you."

"Likewise, honey. Now you go do what you need to do, but remember, you belong here with us."

"I'm not going anywhere, Margie. I'll be back Monday."

"That isn't what I meant."

"What did you mean?" Avery asked, hesitating in the doorway.

"You're not going to California with Grayson Stone? I thought if he asked, you'd go."

"He hasn't asked and even if he did, my answer

would be a definite no. I have no intention of leaving Pleasant."

Avery stepped out of Margie's room and wandered down the hall to her office. The picture of Quinn, the one she'd hidden from Grayson, was still behind her diploma. She pulled it out and set it back on her desk where it belonged. She stared at it for a moment, smiling at the image of her daughter, so like Grayson. She'd loved Quinn from the moment she'd been born. Actually, she'd loved her before she was born.

She'd been a frightened nineteen-year-old when her daughter came screaming into the world but she'd taken one look at her and she'd fallen in love. From that moment on, only Quinn mattered. Everything she'd ever done, she'd done for Quinn.

Letting Grayson in her life? That was also for Quinn. It hadn't hurt as much as she'd thought it might. But that was only because she wouldn't let him into her life enough to hurt her.

"Hey, why the frown? I mean, I know you don't like the way we remodeled, but it isn't all bad." Laura stood in the door of her office. "Mind if I come in?"

"Come on in." Avery welcomed her friend. "How are you doing?"

"Oh, I'm good. My house is still standing." Laura cringed. "Sorry. That's probably a sore spot with you."

"It's fine. I'm still going to build. It's just going to take longer than I thought. I'll have to recoup all the money that my contractor stole from me."

"I wish there was something that could be done about that guy."

Avery shrugged it off, although it still hurt that she'd been duped. "I know. Live and learn."

"Something like that. How's Quinn feeling?" Laura pulled out a chair and sat across from her.

"She's much better. It's been tough, not being able to be at home. I think we're moving back to Nan's in the morning."

"Has it been tough, staying with Grayson?"

She had to think on that one. "Not really tough. He's been gone a lot, helping people in the community. He's an architect and a builder so he's doing what he can for people around town and also for the church."

"That's nice of him. Who would have guessed that Mr. All Hat would be the kind of guy to pitch in and save a community?"

"He isn't saving anyone. He's helping." She heard the snappish tone in her voice and immediately apologized.

Avery glanced at the clock on her desk. "I have to run and get Quinn. She's with Nan, working on a boat. I told Grayson I'd meet him at two. He wants to show me what he has planned for my house."

"Avery, he seems like a nice guy," Laura said.

"He is a nice guy," Avery agreed. "But he's a nice guy who isn't staying in town. He's going to help me get my house started again. And in a few weeks he'll go back to California. Hopefully, once he's there, he won't forget he has a daughter in Missouri. That's really my biggest concern."

Laura gave her a quick hug. "I know you didn't ask for my opinion, but he doesn't seem like the kind of guy who would walk out on his daughter."

Avery nodded. "You're right. I know you're right."

In her head, she knew Laura was right.

But her heart was too frightened to agree.

* * *

An hour later she'd picked up Quinn and was heading to her home. Or what remained of it. As she pulled up the driveway to what, just over a week ago, had been the frame of their future home, she felt a catch in her throat.

"Mom, it's going to be okay," Quinn said, reaching to hold Avery's hand. "Dad's going to fix it for us."

"Of course he is," Avery said. He was already Quinn's hero.

Avery parked and got out to inspect the work that had been done in the past couple of days. The frame was going back up. There were supplies nearby to finish that first phase of building. Grayson came out from behind the building, hammer in hand and wearing a hard hat. He had a man with him, someone she didn't recognize.

"Avery, I'd like for you to meet Larry Childers. He's going to manage everything here when I leave."

At his words, Quinn's face fell. Avery noticed, and she was glad that Grayson noticed, too. Surely, he understood that their daughter wanted him here forever?

"When are you leaving?" Quinn asked, her expression still pained. "Soon?"

"No, not soon. I mean, in a few weeks. But I'll be back." He looked unsure and it wasn't something Grayson was used to, being unsure.

It wasn't going to be as easy as they'd thought, only being part-time in Quinn's life. But it was all they had. Avery met Grayson's eyes and they both knew it. They'd discussed visits and how he would be able to spend time with Quinn. The planning had all been easy because it hadn't included Quinn's feelings in the mix. No matter how simple they thought it would be to share custody, Quinn would feel the pain of separation.

"Miss Hammons, I want to assure you, I'll do my best work for you. We'll have your home finished and better than you ever thought possible." Larry had stepped forward to shake her hand, not realizing the emotions at play among father, daughter and mother.

"I want to make sure you have a storm shelter, too," Grayson added. The conversation was strained. They could discuss the house all they wanted, but they were also thinking about his departure, about Quinn's hurt feelings.

"A storm shelter would be good," Avery responded, but her gaze still lingered on Quinn. She was walking through the skeleton of what would soon become their home.

"I thought so," Grayson said. "I'm also talking to a man about a pole barn. You'll want a barn."

"Will I?" Avery asked. "I hadn't considered a barn. I'm not sure it's in my budget. I doubt a storm shelter is in my budget, either. Remember, I'm trying to cut back on the amount I'll spend."

Larry Childers walked away, giving them space.

"We'll work it out," Grayson told her.

"Why is Tucker at your house?" Quinn asked. She hurried to climb in the back of Grayson's pickup, standing and peering across the field that separated them from the Stone farm. "He has a horse trailer."

"Does he?" Avery asked, pinning him with a glare. "Why?"

"He, uh…" Grayson stumbled over his words and didn't finish.

"Can we go see what he's doing?" Quinn asked.

"Yes, we can. Hop in my truck." Grayson shifted his attention back to the builder. "Larry, I'm going to run

Quinn over to the house. I'll be back over here in the morning if you want to meet me then."

"Sounds good, boss." Larry gave a brief salute. "I need to head home anyway. I'm going to make a few notes and assess where we need to pick up on things."

"Thanks, man." Grayson held out his hand to the contractor. "I appreciate you doing this for me."

"I'm glad I was available."

"What have you done?" Avery asked Grayson as they walked to their cars.

"Trust me," he said.

She was trying but something about the pleased-as-punch look on his face had her worried.

Grayson drove Quinn back to his dad's place. Avery followed behind in her own car. As he drove, he tried to think of explanations for what he'd done.

He parked next to Tucker's truck and Quinn jumped out, running to see what Tucker had in the trailer. Grayson waited for Avery. She took her time getting out of her car. Took her time walking to meet him.

"What have you done?" She repeated her earlier question.

"I know you're going to be upset. I hope you'll hear me out…"

"A horse!" Quinn squealed. "There's a horse in the corral."

"A horse," Avery whispered. "You got her a horse?"

"I have a lot of birthdays and Christmases to make up for," he said, hoping his face looked all contrite.

She brushed her pale blond hair back from her face and glared up at him with green eyes that warned of danger. He considered telling her how beautiful she was. But that might be the worst thing he could do.

Right now he was perched on a land mine and he knew he'd better choose his words carefully.

"I'm sorry," he said. He watched as Quinn hurried to the corral and the dappled Pony of the Americas he'd picked for her. A POA would always be a good choice for a first horse for a young girl. The gray with a black speckled rump tossed her pretty head in greeting and whinnied. Quinn climbed the fence and leaned to claim the horse in a hug. Tucker stood nearby, talking to her, keeping her distracted from his and Avery's conversation.

"Why would you think this is okay?" Avery asked. "Is it because I agreed to let you help me with the house and now you think you can do anything you want?"

"She asked me for a horse," he said, knowing better than to smile. "I messed up."

"Not in her eyes, obviously." Avery's gaze followed her daughter. Quinn started to climb over the fence into the corral and Avery tried to stop her.

"She's safe," Grayson assured her. "I wouldn't buy her a horse that I didn't trust. Besides, Tucker is right there. If you don't trust me, you trust him, don't you?"

"Grayson, you can't just show up here with a horse. This isn't how I parent and I don't want her to think that every time she says she wants something, it's just going to appear."

"I know, I know," he agreed. "I should have talked to you about it first. I talked to Tucker the other day, and he told me about Flash."

"Flash," Avery said with an eye roll. "Really?"

"Flash is a good name for a horse."

"I don't want to talk about the horse's name."

He wasn't an expert but he guessed there was more to this than the horse conversation. The last thing he wanted was to discuss what he and Tucker had talked about. She'd probably be even more angry about that than the horse. This was one of those situations, where no matter what, he was in trouble.

"You're right," he agreed. He let the conversation drop for a moment. Quinn had scaled the fence and now stood on the other side, her hand on the horse's halter.

"That thing had better be gentle," Nan warned as she joined them.

"Tucker assured me he is as gentle as they come. He was a young girl's trail horse and pleasure class show horse. She moved on to a bigger horse and this guy had to go."

"Why would anyone want to get rid of him?" Quinn asked.

"I don't think she wanted to get rid of him," Tucker explained. "She just knew that he would need more attention. She knew we would find him a good home with a girl who would spend plenty of time with him."

"We'll get your tack. You stay and get to know him," Grayson told Quinn.

He took Avery by the hand and the two of them walked to the barn where he'd left the tack he'd bought the previous day.

"Grayson, co-parenting requires we talk to each other. We don't make decisions without informing the other person."

"You're right, and I won't do this again. It was a spur of the moment decision, but on the bright side, it did make her happy."

"Yes, she's happy. She's a happy and well-adjusted

ten-year-old, Gray." She swiped away a tear. "I want her to stay that way."

All of the things she wasn't as a child. He got it. He'd lived in a big fancy house and he'd never gone without, but his family hadn't been the most functional. There had been plenty of fights, doubts and accusations between his parents.

He had always promised himself that he wouldn't have children if he couldn't give them better than he had, if he couldn't give them a safe and functional home. Avery seemed to have figured parenting out and he wasn't sure if he could.

"I want her to stay well-adjusted, too."

"What are we doing?" Avery nearly whimpered. "I don't want this to be what she sees in us, this fighting and doubting and tearing each other up. I want to trust you, Grayson Stone. I want you to be the dad she needs."

"And I want to be that man," he told Avery in a quiet voice, seeking forgiveness and trust. "I want to be a person you can trust."

Silence held them both captive in the stuffy interior of the barn. Nan and Quinn's voices carried through the door, the happy magpie chatter of his daughter and Nan's calm and reasonable tone. Every now and then Tucker would interject something. Tucker, the responsible, decent one.

Avery listened, her eyes closing.

"Please don't break her heart."

"I'm doing my very best to be the dad she needs me to be." He hooked a finger under her chin. "As much as you don't want this, I'm trying to be the man you need me to be, the man I should have been eleven years ago."

She exhaled softly, inclining her head, a positive

sign, he thought. The last rays of sun shot red and gold through the barn, catching the silvery light of her hair and the softness of her expression. He felt himself falling like the floor was dropping out from beneath him. He couldn't ever remember having felt that way before.

"Don't look at me like that," she whispered, catching her breath.

"I'm sorry. I can't not look at you this way."

He brushed a tendril of hair behind her ear and her eyes closed.

"Grayson," she whispered, soft and breathy as he stepped closer.

He cupped her cheek in his palm and brushed his lips against hers. She whispered his name again, then kissed him back.

"What's going on? Are you bringing the tack or not?" From behind, he heard Nan's voice, taking them both by surprise. "You have a child out here waiting and the sun is setting."

"Thanks, Nan," Grayson said with a laugh as he stepped away from the temptation in front of him. "I appreciate the reminder."

"I bet you do," Nan said sharply.

Grayson grabbed the tack he'd purchased for the horse as Avery left the barn with Nan. He watched them walk away and he couldn't help but smile. She'd kissed him. She hadn't turned him down.

He was an expert at fixing things, at rebuilding what was broken. He had come to town to help his father. But finding out he had a daughter had changed everything.

Avery was more than he had ever expected, and that was something he didn't quite know how to handle.

Yet.

Chapter Twelve

Grayson pushed his father up the ramp at the side of the porch in his wheelchair, even though Mathias grumbled the entire time that he could use a walker. His halting speech lent a cadence to the words that sometimes made them difficult to understand.

Nina waited on the porch, her tiny stature but determined expression meaning business. "Mathias Stone, stop your caterwauling."

"Bossy woman," Mathias grumbled as he made his way across the porch of the old farmhouse.

"This would have been a lot easier in the old house," Grayson mentioned as they entered the front door.

"Sold it," Mathias said. "Too big. Too many…"

"Too many what?" Grayson asked as he lifted his father out of the chair and lowered him into the lumpy recliner next to the window. He handed his dad the remote and stepped back as the elder Stone flipped through the three channels that came in on the aging set.

"I could get you satellite TV, you know," Grayson offered.

"Don't want it," Mathias said. He found an *Andy*

Griffith rerun and settled back to watch. After a moment he looked up. "Too many memories. We didn't want to live there after you and your sister were gone. So we moved to Springfield. We needed a place to start over."

Nina buzzed into the room with a tray holding two plates. "I thought you might be hungry."

She set the tray over Mathias's lap, and handed one plate to Grayson.

"Thank you, Nina." Grayson smiled at the woman.

"I don't want noodles," Mathias grumbled as he stuck his fork into the pasta on his plate. "I want meat."

"Tomorrow," Nina called out as she hurried from the room, on to a new task.

"Dad, please be nice to her," Grayson warned. "We can't afford to lose her."

Mathias scooped up some pasta on his fork and shoved it into his mouth. He chewed slowly and then took another bite. Grayson picked up a napkin and wiped the corner of his father's mouth.

"Don't," Mathias growled.

"Do you want alfredo sauce on your chin?"

"I don't." Mathias swallowed and moved his plate so that it was on the edge of the tray. "But I don't want to be helpless."

"I know you don't."

His father leaned back in his chair. "You can't afford to lose Avery."

"I don't have Avery," Grayson informed his dad.

Mathias chewed another bite of pasta, then pointed to the glass of tea with the straw. "Drink."

Grayson held the glass up for his father to take a drink. The doctor's prognosis for Mathias wasn't the best. They thought Grayson's father had continued to have small strokes. Because of the strokes, he had decreased cognitive ability as well as other health issues. He might not get worse anytime soon. But he wasn't going to get better.

He had aged too quickly, having been too hard on his body with the wrong foods, lack of exercise and heavy drinking. Grayson was more determined than ever not to follow down that path.

Mathias pushed the glass of tea away. Grayson set it on the coffee table and waited, knowing his father had something to say.

"I missed out," his father said. "I worked too much and I was hard on my children. You don't want to live with those regrets."

The words hit him full force. Grayson sat back, whistling as he took in his father's meaning. First, he thought about what the words meant for him. And then he realized what they meant for his father. Mathias Stone was a lonely man with regrets. He'd been hard, difficult and often unkind. He'd expected a lot from the people in his life.

"I'm sorry," Mathias said. "For everything I ever said. Your mother forgave me. I hope you will, too."

"I forgave you a long time ago, Dad."

"I appreciate that," Mathias said.

"Dad, I think you should come to California with me." Grayson said quickly, before he changed his mind. He couldn't believe that was his response to this father and son moment.

"No!" Mathias didn't even take time to think about it.

"I can't take care of you here," Grayson told him. "And you're going to need family. If you come to California, I can take care of you."

"This is my home." Mathias's voice raised a notch. "I was born here. I'll die here." The final sentence was somewhat garbled but Grayson understood.

"Calm down. It was just a suggestion. I'm your son and you should be with family."

"Nina can take care of me," his father said. He pushed at the tray. "I'm done. Take this. And you worry about your own life. Buying ponies. Being the hero. When you leave? What then? What about my granddaughter?"

"I'm not walking out on my daughter," he assured his father.

Mathias swallowed and it took him a minute to continue. He clearly struggled to find the words he wanted to say. Grayson waited, wondering at the change taking place in his heart and probably in his father's. Years of being a Christian had taught Grayson the importance of forgiving. At that moment he felt the hardness in his own heart softening toward the man who was his father.

"Dad, I forgive you."

Mathias's gaze snapped toward him and he was clearly shocked.

"I was angry with you for years," Grayson admitted. "Because you sent me away. But then I realized that you also made sure I had a second chance."

"I wasn't an easy man to live with," Mathias admitted. "Don't follow in my steps."

Grayson nodded. "I know."

"You can't get time back, son."

Grayson took his father's tray and left the room. At the doorway he stopped to look back, at a man he'd spent too many years resenting.

"Let me take that." Nina appeared at his side. "He'll sleep now."

True enough, Grayson's father's eyes had closed and his head drooped.

Grayson followed her to the kitchen. He stood at the back door, watching as Dolly the miniature horse tried to find a new spot in the fence to escape through.

"He doesn't want to go to California." Grayson shrugged. "Can't say that I blame him. This is his home. But he won't be able to live on his own."

Nina dried her hands. "I'll do what I can. I guess if it comes to full-time care, that's more than I can handle but I can be here during the week."

"He isn't going to like the idea of a residential home."

"No, I don't think he will." She smiled. "He might be sick but that doesn't mean he won't still have opinions."

His gaze shifted back to the door and the miniature horse. Dolly was trying her best to get through loose fence. Fortunately, he'd done enough repairs that she couldn't get out, but she'd just pointed out a section of fence he had missed.

"I have to go deal with her. If it was up to me, I'd sell the three of them."

"And that is one of the things he might have a differing opinion on. He loves those ornery animals. He makes me take him out to see them every day."

"Every day?" He had no idea.

"Every day. But that isn't your only problem. That looks like trouble coming up the drive." Nina pointed and he knew what he would see even before he looked.

Trouble didn't seem to be a strong enough word for this situation. And yet, his daughter had come to see him. She was riding up the rutted gravel driveway, her backpack hanging over her shoulder as she bounced along on her bike, a pleased smile on her face.

"I'm going to tighten up that fence and see what my daughter is all about."

"I wish I could help, but I have laundry…" Nina said with a little laugh.

Avery wouldn't be happy about this situation. As a father, he had to remember that there were rules. As a man, he had to remind himself that the last thing he wanted was the mother of his child mad at him.

He texted her their daughter's whereabouts as he walked down the drive to meet Quinn.

"I didn't expect to see you today," he told her in a conversational tone. What he really wanted to do was ask her if she had any idea how dangerous a stunt like this could be. He wanted to tell her she could have gotten hurt, or worse.

"I wanted to see Flash," she said, giving him an uncertain look. In that moment she looked younger than her ten years.

"You can always see Flash, but don't you think you should have called first? Was your mom okay with you riding your bike all this way?"

Uncertainty turned to fear on her face.

"I didn't tell her. She was helping Nan in her workshop. Nan forgot something on one of the boats."

"And you left without telling them?" Just then, his phone buzzed. He glanced down and wasn't surprised to see the text. Avery had been frantic. She'd been about to call the police.

Should he be hurt that she didn't think to call him first? He guessed this wasn't the time to think about hurt feelings, but instead to make sure Quinn knew the dangers of riding off by herself.

"I guess I should call her," Quinn said. She looked up at him, brown eyes swimming in tears.

"Yes, you should." He handed her his phone and did his best to keep the stern father expression in place.

He listened as his daughter talked to her mother, apologizing for leaving without telling her. She cried a little but swiped at the tears, too stubborn or too brave to really give in and cry.

Being a dad wasn't an easy job. He wanted to hug her and tell her everything would be okay, so he did. And then he told her she was grounded from her horse for the next few days. Her expression was crestfallen and made him doubt the wisdom of his decision.

After all, what did he know about this parenting business?

Avery probably broke some laws getting to Grayson's in record time. She ignored all the speed limits, didn't come to complete stops. She couldn't help it. She had to get to Quinn. She had to know why her daughter had left the house without telling her. When she got out of her car at Grayson's, she schooled her features. The last thing she wanted to do was scare Quinn to death.

Quinn approached her, hands behind her back, head down. Contrite. Good, that was a start.

"Quinn…" Avery said.

"I'm really sorry, Mommy. I just wanted to see my horse and I thought you would say no. I didn't think you would want to come over here because we were here all week and you just wanted to be at home."

"You're right about all of those things, except if you'd asked, I probably would have brought you over here.

Maybe not the second you wanted, but we would have made a plan."

"Dad said I'm grounded from Flash for a few days."

"Did he really?" She shot Grayson a look and he raised his hands, unsure, questioning. She nodded because, yes, that had been the right thing to do.

She hugged her daughter. "You have to be honest with me."

Quinn nodded against her shoulder. "I heard you tell Nan that he won't be here much longer. It scared me because I know California is a long way. We can't just drive there or anything."

Avery pulled Quinn closer. "It is a long way but there are these things called planes, you know. You'll get to see him. I'll make sure of it. We'll both make sure of it."

Grayson approached from behind her. He put a hand on Avery's shoulder and she fought the urge to turn to him for comfort, for support.

"Quinn, I won't be gone forever and I'll make arrangements for you to visit me, as long as your mom is okay with it."

Quinn nodded, stoic and trusting. "Okay."

"Could you go in the house and check on the judge for me?" Grayson asked.

"Sure." Quinn gave him a suspicious look but left them alone.

"Since Nina is here, she obviously doesn't need to check on the judge. What's up?"

"I wanted to talk to you about tonight. Tucker asked me to help him haul some bulls to the arena and he wants me to try out a horse he might buy. I know Quinn is grounded, but I'd really like for the three of us to do this together."

"Together."

"You're repeating what I'm saying," he teased.

Yes, she was repeating him. She didn't know how to respond to something that sounded like a date. Since she'd become a mother, she'd aimed to end the cycle of single parenting, abuse, neglect. She had ended it. And now here was Grayson and he wanted to be in his daughter's life. It seemed he also wanted to be in her life. She realized she wasn't so far removed from the teenager.

He wasn't like her father, walking away and never returning. But she had to admit that was always in the back of her mind as a possibility.

"You're overthinking this," Grayson told her. "It's just a rodeo. We'll watch Tucker fall off the new horse of his and I'll feel a little vindicated. We'll have a burger and maybe something fried in too much old grease. Quinn will have fun because the two of us will make sure she has fun. And we'll make sure she's protected. Because I know what you're thinking. I know how small towns gossip. I've been the subject of enough of it to write a book."

"I think they did write a book," she teased. "Or at least a few newspaper articles."

He chuckled and she dropped her gaze, needing a moment of not being trapped in the emotions he stirred in her.

"Let's take our daughter to the rodeo, Avery, and let her chase a calf and try to win some money. Maybe you can talk me into playing cards in the arena until a bull chases me down."

"I might like to see that," she said.

She nodded, agreeing to the plan. She would go with

this man who had always been too handsome for his own good. She would laugh at his jokes, share some junk food with her daughter, and for tonight, they would work at being parents together. For Quinn.

Maybe if they did this often enough, it would become natural for them, to work together sharing her.

"Wait a second." She halted midway back to the house. "What do you mean, vindicated if Tucker falls off a horse?"

He pretended he didn't have a clue what she meant. She had no intentions of letting him off the hook.

"Come on," he said, grabbing her hand. "Let's go tell our daughter the good news."

"Not until you explain what you meant." She planted her feet and refused to budge, even though his hand wrapped around hers in a possessive way that she shouldn't welcome.

"Fine," he said after a moment. "I... I'm maybe the tiniest bit jealous of you and Tuck. He's always been a good, decent person. In our friend group, he was the conscience. He told us when we'd gone too far. And he probably gave me a black eye our senior year, when I called you 'the trailer park.'"

Heat bloomed in her cheeks and she dipped her head so that he wouldn't see her embarrassment. He hooked a finger under her chin and raised her face to his.

"That hurt," she admitted.

"I know, and I'm sorry. You were always better than all of us. You and Tuck, the two of you make sense."

"We're just friends," she assured him. "That's all we've ever been."

"That's more than I've been," he said as he dropped

a kiss on her forehead. "But I'm going to make up for that."

The promise in that statement left her unnerved and she didn't know how to respond. She'd come so far from the girl who used to dream of his love, his acceptance. Now she was a woman with a life that was whole and complete. She had a daughter who was everything to her.

Dreams of Grayson didn't fit into the life she'd built for herself anymore. She didn't need him to complete her happiness.

Quinn raced across the lawn in their direction. Avery took a step back, distancing herself from the tangled emotions that Grayson stirred up. In that way, he hadn't changed. And she guessed she hadn't, either.

"I'm sorry." Quinn spoke as she threw her arms around Avery. "I messed up. Big time."

"Thank you for apologizing but more importantly, don't do it again." Avery kissed the top of Quinn's head, then smoothed back her dark brown hair. Her daughter looked so much like Grayson that over the years it had sometimes been painful to see the similar expressions, to witness tiny bits of personality that she'd gotten from him, even though she'd never met him.

"I love you, Mommy." Quinn hugged even tighter.

Avery and Grayson's gazes met over the top of their daughter's head. Avery hugged Quinn and then laughed.

"I love you, too. You're still in trouble," she assured Quinn. "Your grounding will start tomorrow. But tonight we're going to take you to the rodeo."

"All three of us?" Quinn jumped back.

"Yes, all three of us," Avery said. "We need to go

home and get ready. Will you pick us up?" she asked Grayson.

"Yes, I will. Probably about six. Is an hour enough time for you all to get ready?"

"Plenty of time," Avery answered even as Quinn was tugging on her hand.

"Can I stay?" she asked.

"Nope, you're going home with me. Remember, you're grounded."

"Right, grounded. But we're going to the rodeo, so that's awesome." Quinn's face glowed as she looked from Avery to Grayson. The look of a girl whose dreams were coming true.

The look frightened Avery. She didn't want Quinn to get the wrong idea about her and Grayson. She didn't want her own heart to get sidetracked, either.

For tonight, though, they would be a family, and she didn't want to ruin that for Quinn.

Chapter Thirteen

When they arrived at the rodeo grounds Grayson parked his truck and the trailer of bulls he'd hauled for Tucker. That had been a last minute thing. He'd picked Avery and Quinn up shortly before six and then they'd driven over to Tucker's place to hook up the trailer of bucking bulls.

They exited the truck cab, and Tucker headed their way. Tucker was old-fashioned country, a big guy, tall and broad across the shoulders. Grayson was man enough to admit that Tucker was the kind of man that a woman would want to date, probably marry.

"Thank you for hauling them over here," Tucker said. "They're about to start the opening ceremony. Quinn won't want to miss that. If you trust me with your keys, I'll unload the bulls."

Grayson handed him the keys. "Do you need help?"

"Nah, I've got Shay, not that she enjoys helping, and I've got a high school boy that I hired."

"Yell if you need anything."

"Sure thing." Tucker tossed the keys up in the air,

caught them and dropped them into his pocket. "Catch up with you all later."

Grayson steered Quinn and Avery toward the risers where spectators were seated. Some people had brought lawn chairs and were seated in the grass; others stood to watch. The emcee announced the opening ceremonies were about to begin. A young woman on a flashy palomino entered the arena and took a few laps with the Missouri state flag. The crowd came to their feet with a cheer.

The next rider came out on a dark bay, an American flag held high. She circled the arena and came to a stop next to the palomino. Both riders took a lap around the arena together and then returned to the center as the national anthem began to play.

Still standing, the crowd sang along with the young girl performing from the emcee box above the livestock pens. It was a moving experience, even for Grayson, who had experienced it often during his youth. He hadn't appreciated it back then. Today as he stood and really listened to those lyrics, he felt a connection with his country and this community. When the song ended, and a different singer began to sing "God Bless America," he might have teared up a bit.

Then they were asked to bow their heads for the prayer.

"Who knew?" Avery whispered after Pastor Wilson finished praying.

"Who knew what?" he asked as he cleared his throat and they all sat down.

"That you're a sap."

"I'm not a sap, I'm patriotic," he defended himself,

but he saw the twinkle of humor in her expression. "By the way, did you notice we're the talk of the town?"

A flush of pink rushed into her cheeks. "I'd rather not be the talk of the town, thank you very much."

With that, she motioned for Quinn to sit between them.

He grinned at the move and allowed her to do as she pleased. If it meant she stayed with him instead of hightailing it off to sit somewhere else with someone else, he was okay.

As the barrel racing event started, Quinn captured his hand and squeezed it briefly before letting go.

"I love barrel racing so much. Dad, do you think I could barrel race with Flash? Would he be able to do this?"

Avery gave him a bit of a smirk. She knew he couldn't deny Quinn. But he had to be honest. He couldn't just go out and buy her a barrel horse. That would be foolish. She'd be spoiled.

"I don't know that Flash would be much of a barrel horse," he answered truthfully. "He's been trained for pleasure classes."

His daughter seemed slightly disappointed with that response.

"Oh," she said.

"But we could try," he went on. "I'll get some barrels." He looked to Avery. "Is that okay?"

He guessed from her expression that he should have asked her first.

"It's okay," she agreed.

"I'm going to go get a burger." He stood as he said it. "Anyone else hungry?"

"Me!" Quinn said with enthusiasm.

"I thought you all might be ready to eat. Avery, want to help me?"

"Help?" she said.

"Carry food."

Grayson motioned her to go on ahead of him down the steps of the risers. On the way, a few people called out to them, greeting them as if it wasn't a surprise to see them together. They made their way around the arena to the cook shack where burgers were sizzling on the grill outside and a few members of the saddle club worked inside the concrete block building, taking orders and making up the sandwiches.

He spotted Tucker parked a short distance from the cook shack. With a wave Tucker left the group he was with and headed in their direction.

"What do you think, Quinn?" Tucker asked. That's when Grayson realized their daughter had followed them.

"I think Flash should be a barrel horse," she said with all the enthusiasm of a ten-year-old.

Tucker arched a brow and then inclined his head in the direction of the window where they needed to place their order. "You're up. And I can help her out with the barrels. I think Flash will do anything she asks."

"That's what I'm afraid of," Grayson admitted.

Grayson got distracted from the conversation by Avery. She'd asked for something and the woman inside the cook shack giggled and took her money, giving her a form to fill out in return.

"What are you doing?" he asked.

She wrinkled her nose at him. It was about the cutest nose he'd ever seen. He thought she might be all he ever wanted in his life.

"Calm down and just be glad you didn't wear your shiny boots tonight." She gave his dusty work boots a pointed look. "As a matter of fact, tonight you actually look like a boy from Pleasant and not a city slicker with no idea how to tell the front end of a bull from the business end."

Tucker guffawed. Loud, noticeable, attention drawing. "Every end of the bull is the business end. Even Grayson knows that. What are you up to?"

Sugar was sweet but the look on Avery's face was sweeter. Her eyes sparkled as she gave the form back to the woman inside the building.

"I knew you wouldn't sign yourself up and I wanted to make sure you didn't miss your opportunity to play cards with a bull."

"You really want to get back at me, don't you?" he asked her.

"Here's your burgers, chips, drinks and fried cakes." The woman inside the cook shack pushed a couple of boxes their way.

"I mean, I don't want you hurt," Avery said. "But I do want the fun of watching you run from the bull."

Tucker pounded him on the back. "Godspeed, my friend. Godspeed."

"That's it? That's all you're going to say?" Grayson asked the other man as they started to part ways.

Tucker grinned. "Run fast."

They left Tucker and returned, with food, to their seats in the bleachers. Quinn had hurried ahead of them and a friend had joined her. They had a brief conversation but at their arrival the girl hurried back to her own family.

"Who's your friend?" Grayson asked.

Quinn gave the most subtle roll of her eyes as she thanked him for the food he handed her. She immediately popped a crinkle-cut French fry into her mouth. "That was Sara," she said between bites.

"Oh," he responded, not knowing what he was now required to do with the information he'd sought.

"Sara goes to our church but her family doesn't live in Pleasant," Avery informed him.

"Parenting isn't for the faint of heart," he whispered. "Am I not supposed to ask about her friends?"

Avery lifted a slim shoulder. "It's definitely good to know your child's friends."

"Thank you," he answered. "I'm glad I have you to show me the ropes. You're a good mom, Avery."

"I try very hard," she said. "It isn't…"

She stopped talking, and pretended she was busy eating.

"Isn't what?" he prodded.

Quinn asked if she could go sit with Sara for a few minutes. Grayson answered for Avery. "Go right ahead. But stay where we can keep an eye on you."

Quinn took her food and climbed the few steps down to the end of the row of bleachers to sit by Sara.

"Now that we're alone…" he said. "Isn't what? If you have something to say, Avery, say it."

"Parenting isn't easy, Grayson. It isn't rodeos, horses and fried cupcakes. It's being there when she's having a bad day, staying up all night when she's sick, losing sleep when you know you can't pay the bills and still buy groceries. Parenting is tough."

"Have you ever lost sleep over unpaid bills?" he asked. Had Avery and Quinn gone without groceries?

"When I was in college things were tight."

"I'm sorry."

"I didn't tell you that to make you feel bad about the past. I'm telling you because I don't want you to think parenting is always fun and games."

"I know it isn't. I also know that you still don't trust me. I'm doing my very best to change your mind about me. Give me a fighting chance. Please."

"I'm trying," she said with a look that made him wonder if he'd ever win her heart. And he wanted to. He wanted her to trust him enough that he didn't have to beg for, borrow or steal her love.

He was working on it.

Avery ignored Grayson for a few minutes so she could get her equilibrium back. He'd always been able to charm her with a look or the right words. The trouble with Grayson was that he'd rarely meant the things he said.

She knew that this Grayson wasn't the same person. He'd grown up. He'd changed. He deserved a second chance, or at least a chance to have a relationship with his daughter.

As long as he remained truthful and didn't break promises.

Quinn reappeared at her side, snuggling in close. "The bull rides are next!"

"Our favorite," Avery said, wrapping an arm around her daughter's shoulder.

The bull rides, of course, were a crowd favorite. The first ride had Quinn on her feet. Avery pulled her down so she wouldn't block the people behind them from being able to watch. Next to her, Grayson laughed.

"Admit it," he said. "This was a good idea."

She grinned at him. "It was."

The metal gate of a chute clanged open and the next bull and rider spun into the arena. The rider whipped left and then right as the bull spun and bucked. Eight seconds seemed like an eternity. The buzzer finally rang and the rider unwound his hand from the bull rope and jumped off. The bull spun back around and went after him. The rider dodged the hit and ran for the fence while bullfighters jumped in the path to distract the animal.

Quinn grabbed hold of Avery's arm while still bouncing up and down. She settled once the bull lost interest and headed for the exit gate.

"That was intense," Avery said.

"It's a tough sport," Grayson responded, realizing that somehow her hand had found its way into his.

She pulled it away and said, "You at the card table, that's what I'm looking forward to."

"You just want to see me get hurt," he teased.

"No, I don't want you hurt. I only want to enjoy seeing you run around the arena."

They were sitting shoulder to shoulder and she thought he might lean in and kiss her. The instinct to draw back, to protect herself, didn't kick in. It should have. Fortunately, the emcee announced the card game would take place after bull riding and all participants should report to the emcee stand.

"I guess that's me," he said as he leaned away from her. "Say a prayer. I haven't run from a bull in a long time."

"Don't you have bulls out in California?" she teased.

He smiled at that. "Nope. Not on my place. Only horses."

His place. The place that was two thousand miles

away. The place that seemed mysterious and so different from their lives here. She felt herself being pulled into his life and she didn't know how to stop it.

The bull rides continued and Avery somehow managed to keep her mind on the event. With Quinn at her side, bouncing up and down, ducking, cringing, it was easier.

After the last ride, a few men hurried into the arena with a card table and several folding chairs that they set up in the center. Five men, including Grayson, were putting on the Kevlar vests that protected bull riders. It suddenly became real, what she'd done to him. She'd put him in that arena to face a bull.

He was the father of her child. He shouldn't be in there, putting himself at risk.

The emcee started to announce the rules of the game. Each man would sit at the table, both hands on the table. A bull would be turned loose. The object of the game was for the bull to terrorize the card players until they got up and ran. The last one sitting at the table won the prize.

Acting on instinct, Avery started to stand up and tell Grayson not to do it. Then she saw Tucker heading her way. He was a real-deal cowboy with his big grin and dimples, his hat pulled low.

They'd gone out and she'd considered what it would be like to be married to someone like Tucker. He would never let a girl down. He was the kind of man who had taken in his rebellious teen niece. He attended church weekly, sang in the choir. Tucker was all things good.

He'd never been the man for her.

"I have to stop him," she told him as he slid into the space next to her.

His expression shifted, shadowed. His smile dissolved. He wasn't jealous; she knew that. More likely, he was concerned. He, too, had a past with Grayson.

"You know, he isn't going to be pulled out of that arena now that he's in there."

"I don't want his daughter to watch him get hurt."

"Of course not." He said it with a casual drawl. "He won't get hurt. It isn't his first time. You know that, right?"

"I do know that. But he isn't one of us anymore. He isn't from Pleasant."

"No, that he isn't. But it isn't like we can't dirty him up and bring him back to the good life."

"I don't want him to come back," she muttered. "I just want him to be alive for Quinn."

A chuckle rumbled low in Tucker's chest. "Come on, mama bear, I'll help you out."

But they were too late. The emcee announced the name of a bull. Church's Wild Child. Tucker's bull. The bull, a brahma cross, came trotting from a chute at the back of the arena. The mottled gray-and-black bellowed and circled proudly around the arena. The bullfighters, in their clown makeup and cutoff pants, hurried to get the animal's attention and guide him to the men seated at the card table. Including Grayson.

He sat at the end, his hat pulled low, his hands on the tabletop. He didn't look at all nervous. He looked like a man having the time of his life. That made her angry. Here she was, actually afraid for his life. And there he sat laughing and chatting with the other men.

"Stupid men," she murmured. She unclenched her hands when she realized her nails were biting into her palms.

"You're the one who signed him up for this, aren't you?"

"Stop lecturing me. You're supposed to be my friend."

He gave her a gentle smile. "Yeah, I'm your friend. I guess someday I'll be his best man. Not sure how I feel about that."

"Best man?"

"At your wedding," he said without his customary grin.

"I'm not marrying him," she nearly shouted but then she lowered her voice. Quinn was still sitting by her friend but it was possible she might overhear. "He's Quinn's dad and that's it. End of story."

He gave her a careful look and nodded. "Okay, sure. Keep telling yourself that, Avery."

She watched as the brahma bull charged the table and the first card player fell. The man jumped and ran for the arena fence, climbing up and over as the bull tried to catch him.

Grayson remained seated, a wide grin slashing across his face. Men. How could he think this was fun? It wasn't at all entertaining. It was frightening. She shifted in her seat, looking over at Quinn and making sure she was not worried.

While her back was turned, the crowd cheered and then they gasped and went silent. The bull made contact with one of the men seated in chairs. It was Grayson, she realized. She jumped to her feet as he flew to the ground and the bull did a circle around him, pawing the ground and then backing up as if to go at the downed cowboy a second time. Bullfighters intervened and drew the animal away. The man on the ground didn't move and it seemed, for a moment, that neither did Avery's heart.

"He's hurt," she said. "Tucker, he's hurt. Get him out of that arena."

Tucker went running down the steps of the bleachers.

She turned to get Quinn but her daughter had already moved to her side. Quinn's face was bleached white and her eyes were huge. Avery caught her up in a hug.

"He's fine. Tucker will make sure he's okay. Come with me."

Avery led her down to the arena as the emcee spoke in quiet tones and the crowd remained hushed. They were praying. She could hear the low murmurs. She'd been to this arena enough times to know what the crowd sounded like when everyone prayed. She also knew that there would be an ambulance waiting in the back of the arena. Just in case.

Tucker met them as they headed for the gate at the back of the arena. A medic had Grayson on his feet. She watched as he shook off his hat, waved it at the crowd and then settled it back on his head. She rolled her eyes. Always the showman.

"He's fine," Tucker told her. "He got hit pretty good but he'll be okay. He's on his feet and he's talking."

"I'll be the judge of that," Avery told him sharply. She let out a breath as she realized what she'd done. "I'm sorry, Tucker. Could you look after Quinn for a while?"

"Sure thing," he said. "Come on, Quinn. Let's go grab a seat."

As she hurried away, Avery heard him talking to her daughter. He had a calm, reassuring voice. She'd always liked that about Tucker. He'd been her friend when she had few friends. And that mattered. His friendship and his loyalty mattered a great deal to her.

She reached Grayson just as he and the medic got to the ambulance.

"We need to get you checked out at the hospital," she told him.

"I'm not going to any hospital," he grumbled at her. "Avery, I'm fine. I just got the wind knocked out of me, that's all. I don't even have a bump or a bruise."

"Let me take a look," she said. Her first mistake was placing her hand on his cheek. She pulled her hand back and turned to the medic. "Do you have a flashlight?"

He handed her a small penlight. She did a quick examination of Grayson's pupils and handed the light back to the medic.

"Do you remember what happened?" she asked him.

He leaned a little closer and his lips grazed her cheek. "You tried to get me killed?"

She laughed at that, then put a hand on his chest to push him away.

"I was going to stop you but it was too late."

"I'm just teasing," he said with a lopsided grin. "Relax, I'm okay. I'm just sorry I didn't win."

He leaned over to speak to the medic who stood behind her. "Curt, could you give us a sec?"

"We don't need a sec," Avery said, putting space between them.

"Yeah, we do."

"I'd rather just go home," she told him. "Quinn is waiting for me."

"I'm going to find a way for this to work, Avery," he whispered close to her ear.

"Don't." She shook her head and tried to push him away. He held on to her hands with his own.

"I have to. We're a family, the three of us."

"Last week you told me you didn't trust yourself enough to be the person we need."

"I'm working through that." He grinned. "I'm starting to see that I'm pretty trustworthy."

"Grayson, you don't love me." She wished life were different. It was what it was. "I don't love you, either. When I was a teenager, I needed your love, but it wasn't about you. I just needed love. I needed someone to care about me and care for me. I was lost and lonely and hurting. I was angry. But I'm not that person anymore. I'm happy with my life. I have Quinn, and Nan, and God. He never lets me down. He is always faithful and always present. I know what love is and I'm content."

"It's hard to compete with God," he said. "And I'm not sure it's even right to try. But remember this, Avery. We have a daughter together. And I think that matters. A lot."

He touched her cheek, his hand rough and gentle, all at the same time. He pulled her slightly forward to touch his lips to hers. She moved closer without even thinking about it. His other hand touched her waist and he dragged her into the kiss. Her hands found their way to his neck, to the corded muscles, the soft line of his hair.

She didn't love him and she didn't need him. She hoped if she kept repeating that mantra, her heart would believe it and he wouldn't be able to hurt her.

Slowly, he pulled away but then he returned, brushing his lips across hers a second time. She'd lost her mind. In his arms, she always lost herself.

Finally, she broke the kiss. "No."

"No kissing or no to us?" He winked but she thought she saw hurt in his expression.

"Both." She took a deep breath. "I'm very careful about my relationships, Grayson. And I definitely don't kiss men at rodeos while she's watching. This is why I need boundaries, because you make me forget what is important."

As she said the words that were meant to put distance between them, she knew it was as much to remind herself as to warn him.

Her head might hear the words. But her heart was something else entirely.

Chapter Fourteen

Tilly's on a Saturday morning was the place to be. The café was crowded with locals and a few out-of-towners heading to the river. Grayson forked up a bite of biscuits and gravy. Becky, the morning waitress, appeared at his shoulder with the coffeepot, but he waved her off.

"I have to leave in five minutes," he told her.

"Why are you rushing out of here? A man ought to enjoy his biscuits and gravy," Becky teased.

He started to answer but the chair across from him scraped the wood floor. He wasn't surprised that Tucker had joined him. Not surprised but maybe a little annoyed.

"Good morning," Tucker said, his gray eyes too amused for early morning. "How you feeling today?"

"I'm not seventeen anymore and I probably should have more sense than to tangle with bulls," he said. "But it seemed like a good idea at the time."

"When we were kids you were always doing one of two things."

"Really, and what were those two things?"

Tucker's brow furrowed, and then he grinned. "You

had a bad habit of either annoying her or trying to impress her. Last night was not impressive."

Ignoring him, Grayson glanced at his watch. "I have
to go. I'm meeting a delivery truck at Avery's house.
And the cabinet builder."

He pushed to his feet and Tucker did the same. The
other man had several inches on Grayson. "Okay, I
won't beat around the bush. If you hurt either of them,
I'm going to be your worst nightmare," Tucker said,
glaring at him.

"Unoriginal and unnecessary, but thanks for the
warning. At least I know where we stand." He grabbed
his hat off the table and pushed it down on his head but
didn't walk away because he had stopped being that
man a long time ago. "I want your friendship, Tucker.
And I wish you'd trust me. I don't want to hurt her or
Quinn. I've been building a new life for myself for the
past eleven years. Two of those years were pretty tough,
I'll admit. But the last nine, I've managed to stay clean
and sober." He headed for the cash register to pay for
his breakfast. Tucker, not surprisingly, followed.

Tucker tossed a bill on the counter. "I'm buying."

"Not necessary, but thank you." Grayson waved to
a couple of locals as he headed for the door.

"Well?" Tucker asked as they stepped outside into
bright early-June sunshine.

"Well what?" Grayson said, but knowing full well
Tucker wanted more of an explanation.

He sighed then said, "There are a whole lot of un-
knowns in this situation. First, I live in California. That
makes it tough to be the dad Quinn needs. Second, I
wouldn't want to mess up and hurt them."

Tucker stuck a toothpick between his teeth and

chewed on it for a second. "The distance thing is something you and Avery will work out. I guess you could
always move back to Missouri."

"I don't think I can. I have a business, a home, and
Missouri owns too much of my past."

"What does that mean?"

"It means there are people here who would like nothing better than to pull me back into the past."

Tucker readjusted his hat and lifted a shoulder a little
too casually. A guy like Tucker wouldn't get it. Tucker
had never wandered too far off the straight and narrow.

"Trust yourself, Grayson. Trust God that when you
feel like the past is tugging at you, He's going to be
right there with you."

"You're right. I know you are. But living it is a lot
harder." He scanned the street as he adjusted to the conversation and the honesty. "Do you want to meet me
at the building site? I'll show you what I'm planning."

"I'd best get back to the river. We're putting about
thirty canoes in the river today and if I'm not there,
some of my staff can't seem to figure out the river from
the road."

"Have fun with that." Grayson tipped his hat, cowboy style, and headed for his truck.

He drove along the river road, the hill on one side and
the river on the other. It could have been pulled from
a painting, especially with the morning sun seeping
through the trees with splashes of golden light. He loved
his home in California. He'd gotten used to a different
life than the one he'd had growing up. He worked hard,
owned a few acres, a few horses and had made some
good friends. He loved the golden tones of the valley
just twenty miles inland from the coast.

He hadn't missed his home state too much over the years, but being here now, he liked it a little more. When he left this time, he would have something—and someone—to miss.

He pulled off the road and headed west, leaving the foggy river bottom behind and driving through hilly farmland, the grass green from spring rains. Before long he'd have to leave it all behind. He had a decent manager and good supervisors for his business. That didn't mean the company could run itself.

He turned down the graded dirt driveway that led to the building site where Avery's house would stand one day. He was surprised to see her car parked in the parking space on the side of the house.

Avery stood next to the driver of the building supply truck and she didn't look happy. He knew it wouldn't be pretty, explaining to her what he'd done.

He joined the two, waving to Nan, who stood a short distance away, wearing gloves and knee-high farm boots. She looked as if she'd come prepared to work. He wondered where Quinn was at.

"What's going on?" he asked, as if he didn't know.

"This gentleman—" Avery smiled at the driver "—says he is here to deliver building supplies for my home. The funny thing is, I don't remember ordering supplies."

"I ordered them," he admitted. No sense beating around the bush.

"I don't need your building supplies," Avery argued. "I have a plan for how I can make the house smaller and get everything done within my budget."

"Why don't we talk in private about this?" he told her, waiting for her to agree.

She looked from the driver to Grayson, then finally she nodded. "Okay, let's talk privately. Excuse us."

Grayson walked with her through grass that had been recently cut. She must have done that.

"Where's Quinn?" he asked.

"With your father. As soon as we got here, she hightailed it across the field to visit him and the animals. And her horse. I never thought of that being a draw for building here, but now…" She shrugged. "I like the idea of her having him in her life."

"I do, too. And that's probably as much a surprise to me as it is to you. I'll feel better when I leave, knowing he's next door. Knowing you're here for him, too."

"When is this leaving taking place?" she asked.

"Not for a while. Maybe a month. But we have to discuss the house. I've drawn up a plan and I've figured the extra costs for the home I'd like to help you build. I also figured ten years of missed child support payments."

"You don't owe me anything, Grayson."

"I know you think that. But Quinn is my daughter, too, and I have a responsibility. Not just for today and the future, but for what I've missed out on. I should have been able to help from day one."

"I understand," she said. "Listen, this is more about you taking control and not asking. You are a little bit like a dozer that runs over everything in its path. Ask me. Talk to me. I don't like these surprises because they feel as if you're taking over. I'm pretty independent."

"Got it and I apologize."

They walked a bit farther and she stopped. "Thank you."

"Is that you accepting my help?" he asked.

She gave a quick nod. "It is. I accept your help as long as you accept that you have to discuss things with me."

He took the opening she'd given. "Would you meet with the cabinet guy? He's actually going to be here in about fifteen minutes."

"I'll meet with the cabinet guy," she agreed.

The acceptance surprised him, making him feel pretty okay with life. Maybe the choices he'd been making, pursuing, were the right ones after all. He'd prayed about it; he'd sought the open doors and he realized doors were opening.

Something as simple as her agreeing to see the cabinet guy he wanted to hire was evidence of steps forward. They walked back to the house together just as the cabinet guy was pulling up.

"I heard you got taken down by a bull. How are you feeling?" Nan asked with a teasing glint in her eyes.

"I'm a little on the sore side today," he admitted.

Avery chuckled, then covered her mouth with her hand. "Oops, sorry."

"You should be," he shot back but he couldn't keep from smiling. "You're the one who's responsible for my injuries."

"I didn't really mean for you to get hurt."

"You two are a sight and you don't even see it, do you?" Nan shook her head and waggled a finger. "I hope you figure it out before it's too late."

"What does that mean?" Avery asked.

"Oh no, I'm not getting in the middle of it. I have to take Quinn to softball practice."

"To softball practice?" Avery asked. She glanced at her watch. "Nan, she doesn't have practice today. Unless you know something I don't."

Nan looked puzzled. "Well, maybe I got the wrong date. That girl has so many things going on, I'm not sure how you keep track of everything."

"Right now the only thing she has going on is riding Flash." Grayson pointed to the field.

"She saddled him without asking!" Avery started to head for the fence.

Grayson stopped her. "She's doing fine. And I'm sure my dad and Nina were with her."

Avery visibly took a deep breath and let it go. "Right. She's fine."

"I'll head that way and keep an eye on her," Nan offered. "I told Nina I would help her with the garden. She said something is getting the lettuce. Probably rabbits."

"Thank you," Avery called out to her foster mom as Nan walked away from them. She watched Nan for a moment and then turned to Grayson. "Okay, next on the list, cabinets."

That was trust, he realized. It was a simple thing that she'd done, or a few things. Letting him help with the house and trusting his judgment concerning Quinn and the horse. Simple things could be building blocks for a future. Together.

As long as he didn't mess it up.

Avery stood at the tailgate of Grayson's truck, looking over the samples the cabinetmaker had brought with him. There were all shades of brown, white, black, wood stain and a dozen popular colors. How was she ever supposed to make a decision?

"What do you envision?" The cabinetmaker asked. "Close your eyes and picture your kitchen, your bathroom cabinets."

"White," she said after a minute, thinking about how it would look. She could picture the kitchen window in her mind's eye, with the view of the distant hills in autumn, when the leaves would change from green to red, yellow or orange. She sighed. That would be her home.

She opened her eyes and smiled at Grayson. "White, but not flat white."

His eyes twinkled at that. "I knew it. But which color of white?"

The cabinet guy brought out several samples. She picked through them until she found the one that she could see in her kitchen and in her bathrooms.

"Now to design the kitchen," the man said to her.

"This is a lot to think about," Avery said. "I had no idea. I thought I'd pick some cabinets and they would just appear."

Both men laughed at that.

"Okay, this might be why I got taken advantage of," she admitted.

"It isn't," Grayson defended, his expression becoming protective in a way that warmed her heart, because no one had ever, in her life, looked at her like that.

Nan had loved her from the moment she walked into her home as a wild child of fourteen. But Nan's love had always been a given. She'd been a mother to girls who needed a mom. But this look of Grayson's, it lingered somewhere between possessive and protective, and she hadn't realized how much she needed to feel like a person that someone would cherish in that way.

"I'll let the two of you hammer this out," Mr. Bradley said with a gruff voice, clearing his throat as he began to put things away. "I can always come by later in the week and we can go over different kitchen plans.

I promise you, it won't be a chore. I have a fancy computer program that makes it fun and easy."

"Thank you, Mr. Bradley." Avery managed to sound sane, she thought.

Nan must not have thought so. She snorted a little and pulled keys out of her pocket.

"I'm going to check on my granddaughter and the judge."

Then they were alone, the two of them, with too many emotions and too many words to say between them. Avery had done everything to guard her heart, to put up boundaries, to protect herself and her daughter.

Here she stood, wondering why in the world Grayson had to be this person to her. Why did she have to get drawn to him in this way? He was no longer the teen who hurt her with words; he was a man who knew how to be there for her, for his daughter.

"You scare me," she admitted.

He took her by the hand and led her to the tailgate of his truck. The two of them sat together, side by side. Across the field they saw Quinn riding Flash in circles, and it was easy to see the pony's responsiveness to his girl.

He tilted his head to study her. "I'm trying to show you that you can trust me to be in Quinn's life, and in yours, too."

"It isn't that. It's that you've managed to change my heart. I do trust you with my daughter. I do trust you to be in our lives. But when you leave—and you *will* go—I'm going to miss you. That scares me."

"It scares me, too. Because what if someone comes along and realizes what an amazing person you are, and you fall in love with him?" He pulled off his cowboy hat and messed with the brim, shaping it a little as he sat there. "What if you and Tucker…"

She stopped him, her hand on his arm. "Not Tucker. He's just my friend. Nothing else."

She realized she'd admitted so much in a few short minutes. Grayson had also revealed a lot. It was big stuff, she realized. It was a relationship, maybe? But where could this lead them when they were different people and lived their lives so far apart? She couldn't see either of them giving up what they had. So would the newfound relationship only lead to heartache? She thought that there weren't any other possibilities.

Chapter Fifteen

Avery hadn't seen Grayson since Saturday, the day they'd discussed cabinets and the future. On Thursday, her first day off that week, she left Nan with a hug and told her she'd be home by noon. She was supposed to meet Mr. Bradley to go over the design of her kitchen. She couldn't wait to see the house. Nan had been by there and she'd mentioned that it was coming along faster than before. In no time it would actually start to look like a real house. A real home.

"Tell Grayson I said hello," Nan called out as Avery went out the back door.

"I'll tell him." She ran back in to grab her purse. "I might stop by and visit with Nina and the judge. Tell Quinn if she wants to go see Flash to let me know and I'll pick her up after I get finished with cabinets. Unless you need help in your workshop."

"I'll be fine on my own. I have my routine." Nan shooed her out the door. "And if Quinn wants to go ride Flash, I'll give her a ride over there. You go and have a good time."

"Thanks." She waved and ran out the door.

The happiness bubbling out of her couldn't be explained. She told herself it was due to perfect June weather, the excitement of owning her own home and the joy because Quinn had recovered so quickly after the storm.

As she drove to the building site, she did so with her windows down and her favorite Christian group playing on the radio. It was the perfect song about not letting anything or anyone steal what God had given, including joy.

As she pulled up to the house, Mr. Bradley was waiting for her.

"Mr. Bradley, it's so good to see you again. I hope you weren't waiting too long."

"Not at all. I just got here myself. I brought my laptop and we'll see what you like. You'll be amazed by this technology. We'll design your kitchen and you'll be able to walk through it, pick your cabinets, your extras, all of the cool and nifty gadgets. Mr. Stone called me and told me we're not to discuss price."

"Mr. Stone called you?" She was taken aback. "I thought he would be here, too."

"No, I don't think so. He called me a few days ago and told me he had to go back to California."

"He…" Her throat tightened and she had to blink to clear her vision.

"Miss Hammons, are you okay?"

"I'm fine. Of course, I just forgot that he wouldn't be here." The lie didn't come easily. The pain of shattered trust brought a quick flash of tears to her eyes.

"I'm not sure if I'm feeling well," she told him. And that was the truth. "Maybe we can do this next week?"

Mr. Bradley looked confused. "I suppose but we do

need to get started soon. I don't think it's a good idea to wait for Mr. Stone. It didn't sound as if he'd be back anytime soon."

"I understand, but I don't think I can do this right now." She averted her gaze and studied the house with its gabled roofline. Windows, porches and big open rooms. That had been her dream and he'd made it come true.

And then he'd left. The way he said he wouldn't leave.

"I really need to go," she told the cabinetmaker. "I'm sorry."

"Are you sure you feel up to driving?" he asked as he followed her to her car.

"I'm sure. I'm just going next door." She managed a smile and hoped it eased his concern. She didn't want this kind stranger to worry about her. "I'm good. I promise."

"I'll call and check on you tomorrow."

"I'll give you my number," she said.

"No need. Mr. Stone made sure to give it to me before he left. He really did want to make sure the process went smoothly. He already paid me the first installment."

"Did he?"

"Yes, ma'am. You go home and rest. I'll call you tomorrow."

She drove away, numb and yet hurting worse than the night when she'd sat at Tilly's waiting for him to show. The night he'd promised her the whole world would know how much he loved her. Eleven years ago they hadn't talked about trust. They hadn't had Quinn, either.

It was supposed to be different now. They were supposed to be different.

She thought back to conversations they'd had the past weeks. He'd mentioned often that they needed to be a family, for Quinn's sake. He'd never mentioned love to her. Not once. And yet, foolish her, she'd been falling hard the whole time.

Fortunately, she hadn't given him the words. That was something to be thankful for.

Her music came on. Her world wasn't falling apart. God was bringing it all together. He was building something good from her own shattered dreams. He was building His dream for her.

The music unsettled her. She couldn't handle it right now. She turned the radio off and drove in silence. Funny how she'd left Nan's feeling as if her whole world was coming together as it should and now everything was falling apart.

Nina was just getting to Judge Stone's. She got out of her car and worry creased her brow when she saw Avery. Nina petted the basset hound and then met Avery midway to the house.

"I need to see the judge." The words came out harsh and painful.

"Of course, come on in." Nina led her through the back door and into the living room where Mathias Stone sat in his old, lumpy recliner that smelled of cigar smoke.

He grinned his lopsided grin and turned off the news.

"Avery, it's good to see you. What brings you over so early?"

"Grayson left?" she asked, already knowing the answer. Why did she have to sound so lost, so hurt?

She sounded like that eighteen-year-old girl who had knocked on his door all those years ago.

She wasn't that girl any longer. She told herself to stand up straight and take control.

"He said he had things to take care of in California," Judge Stone said. "I'm sure he'll be back soon."

"He didn't say goodbye," she said. She regretted the words immediately. "He didn't tell Quinn goodbye."

"Who didn't tell me goodbye?" Quinn asked as she hurried through the front door.

Through the window, Avery spotted Nan's car.

"Isn't Nan coming in?" Avery asked, wanting to change the subject.

"No, she said she had to get back to work. Who didn't tell me goodbye?" Quinn asked but her smile had disappeared. Her face paled as she looked from her grandfather to Avery. "He left?"

"I'm sorry," Avery said. "I know he'll be back."

"When?" Quinn asked. "We were supposed to try barrels at the rodeo with Flash this weekend. That's in just a few days."

"I know it is. I know that Tucker will take your horse for you. You can still ride." Avery reached for Quinn. "It'll be fine. He'll be back."

"But you don't know when."

"No, I don't know when. I'll call him and ask."

"I tried calling him this morning," Judge Stone said. "No answer."

"No answer?" Avery couldn't imagine Grayson not answering his father's call. But then, a few days ago she wouldn't have imagined him leaving town and not saying goodbye to his own daughter.

Her mind took a terrible turn as she remembered him

talking to Greg Butterfield. Once an addict, always an addict, someone had recently told her. Grayson himself worried that he might fall, that he might use again.

The what-ifs ran through her mind and she tried to push the thoughts aside. She made Quinn her focus. Quinn, who looked more shattered, more hurt. This was exactly what she'd never wanted to happen to her daughter. She had wanted to protect her from a father who walked away.

"He'll be back," Quinn said with a shaky smile. "He promised he would always be there for me. Can I use your phone?"

Avery handed her the cell phone from her pocket. "His number is in my contacts."

She watched, knowing what would happen but praying for a different result, praying he would answer. He didn't.

"I'm sure there's a good reason," Quinn assured her, assuring herself. "I know he wouldn't leave without saying goodbye. He must have had a good reason."

"Quinn," Avery started. Her daughter put up a hand to stop her. She was ten and fighting to hold on. She didn't need for Avery to tell her there was never a good reason for a father to leave without a goodbye.

"No. I'm going to ride Flash. My dad will be back. Soon."

Avery agreed; Grayson would be back. But next time around, she would protect herself and her daughter a little more carefully.

Avery went to work the next day and she pretended, or tried to pretend, that everything was fine. She checked on Margie, she played checkers with Daron

Young, she danced with Iva May. Laura watched as she headed for her office, then she got up and followed Avery. "What's up?"

Avery glanced up from her desk. "What do you mean? Nothing is up."

"You've been in a terrible mood all day. You're pale as a sheet. You aren't eating. You're right. That's all very normal."

"He left," Avery finally admitted. It still hurt to say the words.

"Grayson? Mr. All Hat and No Cattle left you?" Laura sat down.

"He left his daughter, not me." Avery was determined to extricate herself from the pain of the situation. It wasn't hers, it was Quinn's.

"Oh, Avery, that's terrible. What reason did he give?"

"He didn't give a reason. He didn't say goodbye. He didn't tell us when he'd be back or what he was doing. He just up and left. He isn't answering his phone. I'm worried he's…"

She didn't want to say it. She had wanted desperately to trust him, to believe him.

"Have you called the police? I mean seriously, this could be a missing person thing."

"He told his dad he had to go back to California. We called the business there and his home. They are unaware of his location and they also have not been able to reach him." She buried her face in her hands. "That's how they say it, like it's a business call and not a worried daughter needing to know if her father is safe."

"I'm sure there's an explanation." Laura tried to sound positive.

"Right, like he was done playing dad. He was done

playing…" She rubbed a hand over her face. "Done playing with my emotions. That's all he's ever done."

"Maybe, but maybe you're wrong. Maybe you've been hurt so many times that you just expect people to walk out on you."

"This feels like walking out. I love him. Why is it I can't learn my lesson when it comes to Grayson Stone?"

"Because he's charming and kind and he helps the elderly and women and kittens."

"And then he leaves."

It came back to his leaving. Always. It came back to Avery always feeling as if she wasn't enough. She hated that feeling and she was determined to never experience it again.

Ever.

Chapter Sixteen

"Where have you been?" Tucker asked as he slammed Grayson against the wall of the cook shack at the Pleasant Rodeo Arena.

Grayson pushed his friend off and straightened his hat. "What's that for?"

"For walking out on them. I warned you not to hurt Avery and Quinn."

Tucker's fist came up and Grayson remembered how much he didn't like having a broken nose. And tonight it was especially important that his nose not be broken. He had business to take care of.

Grayson put both hands up in surrender. "I'm not going to fight you. I'm just asking for an explanation. If you'd tell me how I walked out on Avery and Quinn."

Something wasn't adding up and his good mood began to evaporate under the heated glare of his friend.

"Come on, Tucker, give me a break. I need an answer."

"You left without saying goodbye. You've ignored phone calls. You left your daughter hanging after promising to bring her tonight. But don't worry. I loaded

Flash and brought him. And Nina brought your dad so
he can watch her barrel race for the first time."

"I'm here to watch her, too." Grayson was still lost.
"What do you mean, I didn't tell her I was leaving? I
wrote a note and gave it to Nan. I even left a number
where they could reach me because I knew my cell
phone wasn't going to work."

"You left a note with Nan?" Tucker seemed suspicious. Grayson couldn't say that he blamed him.

"Yes, I left a note. I went by the house. Avery was at
work. Quinn was with a friend. Nan said she'd let them
know that I had to leave town. I wanted to surprise them
but I also wanted them to know I would be back today.
Unfortunately, I had plane delays and couldn't get back
as early as I planned."

"You're going to have to tell Avery all this. And
Quinn. But Quinn first. She's been hurt and angry all
week."

"Where is she?"

Tucker pointed to the horse trailer a short distance
away. His ten-year-old daughter was standing next to
Flash, the horse saddled and bridled and ready to go.
Grayson thanked his friend and headed her way.

She saw him coming and didn't look happy to see
him.

Grayson hesitated, wishing he knew the right words
to say.

"I'm sorry." He started there. "I didn't mean to leave
and have everyone upset. I left a note with Nan, but she
must have forgotten."

"Nan forgets everything," Quinn said as she ran a
hand down her horse's neck. "But she wouldn't forget
to tell me goodbye."

Grayson blinked away tears. "I didn't forget, Quinn. I stopped and let Nan know. You weren't at home. It was important that I go. It was unexpected business that I couldn't ignore."

"It was more important than us?"

"Never. You and your mom, the two of you are the most important thing to me."

"You have a funny way of showing it."

He grabbed his daughter in a hug that she briefly fought but then she leaned against him and cried. "I thought you weren't coming back," she sobbed.

"I promised I would. You have to trust me. I will work night and day to make sure you always know that you can trust me. I'm going to be here for you."

"Why did you have to leave?" she asked.

"It was business. But I need to talk to your mom first. I need to explain to her."

"That's going to be hard to do," Quinn told him. "She's pretty mad at you. I heard her tell Nan that you did what you do best. You left without saying goodbye."

"Well, then, I'm going to have to find a way to convince her that I'm not saying goodbye."

"Huh?" Quinn looked confused.

"You'll see." He helped her on her horse. "Ride over to the gate. I have a surprise for you."

Avery heard the crowds of people shouting and clapping. She had no idea what was going on in the arena and she really didn't care. She'd been helping in the cook shack because they'd been shorthanded. That had meant she was in the back, making pulled pork nachos and passing them over to the ladies at the counter. She was hot, sweaty and really only wanted to get outside in time to watch Quinn.

"Hey, Avery, you have to come out here and watch this. I promise it's something you don't want to miss," Tucker called out as he leaned through the window.

"No, thanks." She made another order of nachos and Linda, the head of the concession stand, told her she was being relieved of her duties.

"I don't mind helping," Avery said.

"We're good. Our second shift is coming in and you need to watch your girl run barrels. Thank you for helping out."

"You're welcome," Avery said. She washed her hands and left through the back door of the building.

Tucker was waiting for her.

"What is wrong with you?" she asked as she tried to skate by him. "I need to go find Quinn."

"She's already in the arena."

"Why is she in the arena? It isn't time for her event yet."

Tucker took her by the shoulders and made her face the arena. That was when she saw him. Grayson Stone on a big gray horse. Quinn was next to him on Flash. Each of them had a pole and they held a banner between them.

"No!" she said. "Absolutely not. He can't come home and pull a stunt like this and get my daughter involved."

"I think you should hear him out," Tucker advised.

"I thought you were my friend."

"I am your friend." Tucker put a hand to her back and moved her toward the gate. "He needs to explain what happened."

"Tucker, I just want to leave. I'm tired, hot and

sweaty. Grayson is sitting out there with a Marry Me sign and he has Quinn holding that sign with him. I can't go out there. I can't let him humiliate me again."

"Trust him." Tucker said it so seriously that it made her stop. "Let him explain."

She walked through the gate that he opened and into the arena to the cheers of the crowd. People she'd known her entire life sat alongside people who didn't even know her name but they all clapped and shouted as Grayson took the sign and dismounted his horse in one fluid, heart-stopping motion.

He strolled up to her while Quinn remained seated on Flash, the pony prancing just a bit as the crowd roared. But Quinn had control. She calmed her horse and sat him with easy confidence, smiling at her mom and her dad.

"What are you doing?" Avery asked as Grayson approached her.

"I came back," he said.

"Good for you. Meanwhile, your daughter thought you'd left for good because you couldn't be bothered to say goodbye. You didn't answer your phone or even text and let us—let her—know that you were safe and that you weren't…"

She swiped at the tears, the stupid tears, and she stared up into his face, noticing the hurt and anguish.

"This might have been a mistake," Grayson said as he glanced around. "It seemed like a great idea while I was planning it."

"Did leaving seem like a good idea, too?"

"I didn't leave." He sighed and shook his head. "I did leave, but I left a note. Nan was the only one at home. I left a note with Nan. I had an urgent business meeting that I had to take care of. It was unexpected and I didn't have time to explain."

"What could be that urgent?" she asked. "And what did the note say?"

"The note promised you that I would be back on Saturday because I wouldn't miss Quinn's first competition for anything. The note told you that I love you and that I would miss you every day that I was gone but when I got home, I'd explain."

She sobbed into his shoulder. "Explain what?"

He held her close. "That's the surprise."

"Tell me the surprise," she ordered. "Seriously, Grayson, I'm standing in an arena with dozens of people watching and I'm not enjoying this."

He had the nerve to laugh. "You're very impatient. But first, I want you to know, I'm serious about us. You, me and Quinn. We're an us. We're not two separate families. I want us, Avery. Together forever."

"How do we do that?" she asked, tears rolling down her cheeks.

"We start by living in the same state," he told her. "I never planned on selling my uncle's business. He left it to me and trusted me with it. But last week I got a phone call from a company that was interested not only in buying my business but my house, too. I took that as a sign that God also wanted there to be an us."

"That does sound as if God had a hand in this," she admitted.

He dropped to one knee and held out a ring. "Avery, I've hurt you. I've let you down. I've let myself down. But I think I'm finally the man I need to be in order to be the husband and father you and Quinn need me to be. Will you marry me?"

The entire arena erupted with dozens of voices yelling, "Say yes!"

She did say yes. And within moments Quinn had joined them. Grayson kissed his soon-to-be wife and pulled his daughter into the circle of his arms. They hugged and kissed as the crowds clapped and cheered.

Avery knew what it was to be loved. She knew what it was to be whole. And now her family was complete.

Almost.

Epilogue

June. One Year Later

Avery and Grayson were married in December, just six months after his very public proposal. They'd married in their church, and Avery had planned her dream wedding, because having Grayson meant she started dreaming again. Her dream wedding had included twinkling lights, white poinsettias and snow.

It hadn't snowed but Grayson had hired a company to produce snow for the happy couple as they left the church building to the tolling of the bells. It had been perfect, romantic and everything that dreams were made of.

Most of all, it had been a moment of celebration with God at the center. That was their plan for the marriage and family they planned to have. They knew there would be tough times, there would be storms to weather, there would be heartache to live through. They also knew that God would guide them, bless them and give them joy, even during the difficult times.

Their house had finally been finished and it was

more than Avery ever thought it could be. It was a little too big, because Grayson always seemed to go too far in his planning. The kitchen was huge. There were four bedrooms and not the two that Avery had originally planned.

More bedrooms weren't a problem, he'd told her. They'd just have to fill them with more children.

Avery was wrapping a package, knowing he'd be home soon. He'd sold his business in California, relocated his horses to Missouri and he'd started a new contracting business in the Ozarks. He'd also invested in Tucker's river outfitters business. His days were busy but he was home each night with Avery and Quinn.

On this evening in early June, the sound of his truck coming down the drive spurred her to action. She hurried to the kitchen, placed the package on the counter, then she stared at the dinner preparations. Grayson was still the better cook, but since her main job these days was to take care of the judge, she found herself spending more time trying to create dishes that her family enjoyed.

"What's for dinner?" Quinn asked as she came through the door. She'd been outside with Flash and declared that he would never be too small for her. Since she was nearly as tall as Avery, that seemed doubtful. But they definitely wouldn't sell him when Quinn outgrew him. Flash was theirs forever.

"We're having taco casserole," Avery said as she pushed the gift back a smidge so her daughter wouldn't see.

"That's my favorite," Grayson said as he came through the door. "Or wait, maybe my favorite is you." He pulled Avery close and kissed her.

"What about me?" Quinn asked.

Her dad picked her up and swung her around. "And you are my favorite daughter."

"I'm your only daughter," Quinn reminded him.

Grayson spotted the gift. "What's that? Is it someone's birthday and I forgot?"

"Not really a birthday," Avery answered.

"Who's it for?" Quinn asked, reaching for the gift.

"Not for you," Avery replied. She took the present from Quinn and handed it to Grayson. "It's for your dad."

Grayson took the gift and gave her a wondering look.

"You bought me a gift?"

She gave him a secretive smile. "Something like that."

He unwrapped it slowly, found the box inside and opened it. Quinn moved close to his side as he pulled a framed picture from the box.

He held it for a moment, studying the photograph, turning it, looking at it for a long time. And then a tear rolled down his cheek.

Quinn took the picture from his loosened fingers as he stepped to Avery and pulled her close.

"Is that a tadpole?" Quinn asked with disgust. "Why would you give him a picture of a tadpole when we have good pictures? Oh wait. Is that…"

"It's a baby," Avery and Grayson said in unison.

"No way!" Quinn shouted. "But babies cry a lot and they're stinky. Did you really think this through?"

Avery couldn't stop laughing, even as Grayson kissed her.

"Thank you for making me the happiest man alive."

"This makes you happy?" Quinn said. "Babies are a lot of trouble."

"Quinn, you're going to have a little brother or sister."

Quinn looked at the picture again. "I mean, that isn't terrible…" And then she wrapped her arms around both of her parents. "Us just got a little bigger."

"Yes, we did," Grayson said, hugging both of them in his strong embrace.

* * * * *

*If you loved this story,
pick up these other books
from much-loved author Brenda Minton*

Reunited with the Rancher
The Rancher's Christmas Match
Her Oklahoma Rancher
"His Christmas Family"
in Western Christmas Wishes
The Rancher's Holiday Hope
The Prodigal Cowboy
The Rancher's Holiday Arrangement

Available now from Love Inspired!

Find more great reads at www.LoveInspired.com

Dear Reader,

I'm so pleased to start this new series set in my home state of Missouri. I grew up playing on the banks of the James River. We caught tadpoles, swam, climbed the river bluffs and spent summer evenings camping under the starlight. As an adult, we still love the river. Camping, fish fries and canoeing are a big part of our lives here in southwest Missouri. For that reason, it was fun to create a series and a community that embodies both the river life and also the farming that is an integral part of our Ozark lives.

I hope you'll enjoy these books set in the fictional town of Pleasant, Missouri. Like many towns that I know, it is a close knit town where neighbors help one another, churches are the heart and the soul of the community and friendships last a lifetime.

Avery and Grayson are complicated characters with a past that must be dealt with before they can trust each other and themselves. As they work to build a relationship that will keep their daughter safe, they learn that life's storms can tear us apart but faith can build us up and keep us strong, even when faced with the unexpected.

I love hearing from readers! Please email me at Minton.Author@gmail.com.

You can also find me on Facebook, where I love connecting with readers: Facebook.com/brenda.minton.

Brenda Minton

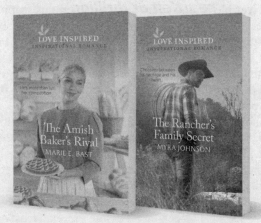

COMING NEXT MONTH FROM
Love Inspired

AN AMISH MOTHER FOR HIS TWINS
North Country Amish • by Patricia Davids

Amish widow Maisie Schrock is determined to help raise her late sister's newborn twins, but first she must convince her brother-in-law that she's the best person for the job. Nathan Weaver was devastated when his wife deserted him, but can he trust her identical sister with his children...and his heart?

THEIR SURPRISE AMISH MARRIAGE
by Jocelyn McClay

The last thing Rachel Mast expected was to end up pregnant and married—to her longtime beau's brother. But with her ex abruptly gone from the Amish community, can Rachel and Benjamin Raber build their marriage of convenience into a forever love?

THE MARINE'S MISSION
Rocky Mountain Family • by Deb Kastner

While ex-marine Aaron Jamison always follows orders, an assignment to receive a service dog and evaluate the company isn't his favorite mission—especially when trainer Ruby Winslow insists on giving him a poodle. But training with Ruby and the pup might be just what he needs to get his life back on track...

HER HIDDEN LEGACY
Double R Legacy • by Danica Favorite

To save her magazine, RaeLynn McCoy must write a story about Double R Ranch—and face the estranged family she's never met. But when ranch foreman Hunter Hawkins asks for help caring for the nieces and nephew temporarily in his custody, her plan to do her job and leave without forming attachments becomes impossible...

THE FATHER HE DESERVES
by Lisa Jordan

Returning home, Evan Holland's ready to make amends and heal. But when he discovers Natalie Bishop—the person he hurt most by leaving—has kept a secret all these years, he's not the only one who needs forgiveness. Can he and Natalie reunite to form a family for the son he never knew existed?

A DREAM OF FAMILY
by Jill Weatherholt

All Molly Morgan ever wanted was a family, but after getting left at the altar, she never thought it would happen—until she's selected to adopt little Grace. With her business failing, her dream could still fall through...unless businessman Derek McKinney can help turn her bookstore around in time to give Grace a home.

LOOK FOR THESE AND OTHER LOVE INSPIRED BOOKS WHEREVER BOOKS ARE SOLD, INCLUDING MOST BOOKSTORES, SUPERMARKETS, DISCOUNT STORES AND DRUGSTORES.

LICNM0621